FAIR WAR

Lord Leigh... ...esist kissing you... ...tical of me to say... ...ain."

"It is my understanding that is not an un-natural state for you," Angel replied. "But do not concern yourself. In all honesty, I found it agreeable."

"Be careful of speaking so frankly," Leighton cautioned. "It could easily be misunderstood, or worse, advantage taken."

Angel was outraged. "You have the audacity to warn me of such dangers? Are you a moral tutor for the rest of the world? If I want to kiss someone back, I shall do so."

"I was only thinking of your welfare," Leighton said.

But at the moment, her welfare was the last thing on Angel's mind. . . .

ROBERTA ECKERT is a registered Interior Designer and an Art and Architectural historian. She attended Albright Art School at the University of New York at Buffalo, and received her BA in Art History from the University of South Alabama. She lives with her husband and family on the Gulf Coast and happily devotes her time to writing Regency fiction.

SIGNET REGENCY ROMANCE
COMING IN AUGUST 1990

Sheila Walsh
The Arrogant Lord Alastair

Katherine Kingsley
A Natural Attachment

Barbara Allister
The Frustrated Bridegroom

LADY ANGEL

Roberta Eckert

A SIGNET BOOK

SIGNET
Published by the Penguin Group Penguin Books USA Inc.,
375 Hudson Street, New York, New York, 10014, U.S.A.
Penguin Books Ltd, 27 Wrights Lane, London W8 5TZ, England
Penguin Books Australia Ltd, Ringwood, Victoria, Australia
Penguin Books Canada, Ltd, 2801 John Street,
Markham, Ontario, Canada L3R 1B4
Penguin Books (N.Z.) Ltd, 182-190 Wairau Road,
Auckland 10, New Zealand

Penguin Books Ltd, Registered Offices:
Harmondsworth, Middlesex, England

First published by Signet, an imprint of Penguin Books USA Inc.

First Printing, July, 1990
10 9 8 7 6 5 4 3 2 1

Copyright © Roberta Eckert, 1990
All rights reserved

 REGISTERED TRADEMARK—MARCA REGISTRADA

Printed in the United States of America

BOOKS ARE AVAILABLE AT QUANTITY DISCOUNTS WHEN USED TO PROMOTE
PRODUCTS OR SERVICES. FOR INFORMATION PLEASE WRITE TO
PREMIUM MARKETING DIVISION, PENGUIN BOOKS USA INC.,
375 HUDSON STREET, NEW YORK, NEW YORK 10014.

To Holly
My fair first-born and loving friend

Prologue

Dear Libby,

I miss you more than words can say. How I should like to be with you to laugh at nothing and everything. To tell you honestly, I even miss Witherspoon's Seminary for Young Ladies. I swear 'tis the truth, for there is little-enough laughter here.

It is not that I'm unhappy: it's just that I am an embarrassment. I see it in the cool appraisal of their beady, little eyes and disapproving, pursed lips. It is a pity that we are judged by our parents. And, Libby, you must admit Mother caused enough scandal to last generations.

Grandfather has tried his best, but you know how tyrannical he can be! He sweeps all opposition aside. What he believes in simply must be what everyone else does.

He dresses me like a princess and has bestowed a dowry half the crowned heads of Europe couldn't match. So you see, I've become very eligible. I imagine the roads to London congested with shabby carriages carrying every available fortune hunter in the realm. The image is amusing, if exaggerated, and is bound to keep me humble, for it will hardly be my charms that create such devotion. This leaves the anxiety of affections out of the question, and judging from Mother's luck at love, I deem that aspect to be an advantage.

I've told Grandfather if it's to be only fortune hunters that seek my hand, then it will be one of my own choosing. I actually don't mind too much, since Grandfather has arranged for my control over the major portion of my dowry monies. Can you imagine the raised eyebrows if that fact becomes known? He has never trusted any man since Mother's escapades.

Don't allow anyone to see this letter. Destroy it! I pretend that nothing is amiss and that I am, by far, the most desirable catch of the Season. I couldn't bear anyone to think otherwise. You can imagine the comments on my hauteur, but it's the only way I'll survive with some pride intact.

You wouldn't believe my decorum. It is so everyone will know I am hardly the *femme fatale* my mother was. How boring! Since I don't really wish to emulate her, I could easily be mistaken for a pious saint. You wouldn't recognize my retiring demeanor.

Come up to London soon and we shall see the sights together. How I wish you could be present this Season. I miss you, for Aunt Mary Beth is hardly someone with whom I could conspire.

Lady Leighton is giving a ball that I am to attend. To think of it, her son is an eligible bachelor, and a marquess too! How desirable though, I question. He is more the rake with plump pockets than a kowtow with pockets to let. I doubt I shall be able to consider him a possible suitor.

My love to you,
Angel

Lady Angel Harlan smiled wryly at her name as she signed with a flourish. It was chosen by her impetuous mother on the declaration that the infant looked exactly like a cherub and, perhaps, in the hopes the name might direct her footsteps. Angel continued to smile, grateful her mother had not gone so far as to name her Chastity or Prudence.

A little furrow appeared on her brow when she folded the letter, for the cavalier words of the missive did not match her sentiment.

1

Lord Anton Stewart, Marquess of Farnham, sat impatiently waiting for his daughter and granddaughter to arrive. He liked punctuality. He was short, rotund, and soberly dressed. He once remarked to his valet, when rejecting a colorful waistcoat, that his girth did not need further attention. A fringe of gray hair circled his head just above his ears like an abbot of old. Fingering his watch fob, he watched the door.

He carried an overt aggressiveness sometimes found in men of small stature. That manner had served his financial ventures, yet often failed him in the success of his relationships with his family.

His timid wife had died following the stillborn birth of his much-desired son. The pregnancy had followed too soon upon the birth of their younger daughter, Evelyn. Never completely recovering from that loss, he buried that disappointment in fierce activity to perfect his landholdings and an overriding need to order all around him to his liking.

This dictatorial manner was surely the reason Evelyn had so flagrantly rebelled from his authority and, later, from the confining life with a dull husband; thereby earning the notoriety of scandal that seemed for some titillating reason to have a life of its own.

Evelyn's foolish actions had been an even greater burden and cause of increased annoyance. It was later, as he raised Angel, that he began to soften, feeling a tender, growing love and commitment.

His imperious manner was too strong to be altered, but the child soon recognized his feelings and twisted him shamelessly around her little finger. Neither was truly aware of this aspect in their relationship, because it was accompanied by genuine regard. And so, if Angel enveigled, Lord Stewart gave willingly.

He watched his granddaughter decorously enter the dining room. He was not fooled by her studied demeanor, and he struggled to hide a smile that was not so easily subdued in his piercing blue eyes.

Mary Beth, looking always like a little brown wren, followed behind. It will do well to have her at Angel's side, he reasoned. One simply could not look at Mary Beth and think of anything but propriety.

"Mary Beth, are the arrangements for Angel's come-out completed?" he asked as soon as they had taken their seats.

"Yes, and I'm sure you'll approve," Mary Beth answered with a cool nod.

"Spare no expense."

"I wouldn't think of it, Father," Mary Beth replied.

Stewart studied his daughter for a moment. An odd one, he thought, never can tell what she's thinking. He dismissed the notion with a shrug.

Turning to Angel with candor, he said, "You're a fine-looking girl, possessing exquisite manners.

You'll have no problem marrying well. The handsome dowry will sweeten the pot," he said in the self-satisfied chuckle of a man with the power to bring about his wishes.

That hurt, Angel thought, to be purchased like some brood mare! How embarrassing! It would take a sizeable dowry to snag her a husband. Angel blushed with chagrin.

The old marquess surveyed his granddaughter with a pang of regret. He knew what she was thinking, and she was correct. It was ludicrous that an event that happened fifteen years ago should be allowed to color her existence. He had raised this girl when Evelyn had run off with that spurious Italian count, leaving husband and Angel behind.

"You'll not be required to marry someone you have a distaste for . . . only one of your own choosing. Choose well! I should think somewhere in all England, there is someone to suit you." He did not mean to sound so gruff. He had actually tried to soften the comments.

"Will he have me?" she asked in a voice barely over a whisper.

"Don't be a ninny. Of course he'll have you. My words may be too blunt. Forgive me. I've lived through the reckless antics of your mother and I'll not do so again. You'll marry sensibly and settle down. I'm old and desire to have you settled. You do understand. You're a good girl. I know you'll agree."

He sent a telling glance toward Mary Beth. She ignored it by taking a little sip of wine.

"Yes, Grandfather," Angel replied with a sinking heart. "My mother married sensibly, then ran away for love. Therefore, I must marry in hopes of erasing her scandal. Am I to forever be the possible iteration of my mother?" The rancor in her voice touched him.

"I've told you what I want. You're fetching, charming, and rich. Our family ranks as one of the most illustrious in all England. Go back to the Normans, we do."

Angel, amused by his choice of "illustrious," smiled.

Lord Stewart returned the smile. He loved her quick mind. Yet he continued his defense. "Name me just any of the hallowed families that bask in their self-importance and I'll show you one that abounds with past scoundrels. Why, the pompous Lady Arlington's father wore the horns so frequently, her brothers and sisters were known as the 'Innominate Assortment.' " He chuckled, but upon hearing Mary Beth's gasp, he had the decency to look embarrassed.

"Shouldn't speak to you in such a manner. But there it is! You might as well know the truth. You'll do just fine. I have no doubt."

Angel smiled in amusement. He never, never missed making his point. Somehow, there was comfort in his directness.

She nodded in agreement. "I shall try to find someone you think is suitable."

With an audible sigh, Angel crossed her bedchamber to stand before the great, mullioned windows. She gazed down upon the glorious spring garden and wished her spirits reflected at least some of the joy the riotous colors seemed to indicate. *How I should like to run barefoot through the clover at Harlan Hall. Never have I missed freedom more, not even at Witherspoon's!*

Grandfather's right; I am acting like a ninny. In truth, a trapped ninny, but a ninny nonetheless.

Where is my spirit? What terrible prospect faces me that doesn't face every marriageable girl in my social circle: to catch the best possible prospect for a husband and settle to raise a family? Some girls lack dowry, some, pleasing looks, and so I have a notorious family scandal to overcome. Self-pity will not serve my purpose. I just wish something would happen!

Angel leaned against the window frame, recalling her interview when Grandfather had first summoned her from school.

A smile turned the corners of her mouth as she remembered the trepidation in which she had entered his library. Temerity was more to her nature, but Angel adored her grandfather, who was a formidable, opinionated, and coercing patriarch. He brooked no fools. One never had to deduce his opinions.

I am not my mother's daughter. No man could ever entice me into some foolhardy venture in the name of love: not even to mention leaving a child behind. Tears stung her eyes for a moment. Somehow the pain of that rejection never seemed to heal.

Enough of these maudlin thoughts, she told herself. Swiftly turning from the window, she smoothed her dress and tucked in a stray curl, as if to bring order to herself and, thereby, her thoughts.

Her action had a delicate quality, for she was slender and stood just two inches over five feet. There could be no doubt of the resolve clearly displayed on her face.

Taking up the cloud of white muslin, chosen especially for Lady Leighton's ball, she held the elegant ball gown to her and stared at her reflection in the cheval mirror. Turning this way and that, she hummed a little tune and matched it with several little dance steps. If the evening proved to match the gown, it would be an unequivocal success. Smiling at this thought, she curtsied to her reflection.

"My, my, our spirits are improving," Aunt Mary Beth said upon entering the room.

Mary Beth always took pleasure in the beauty of Angel's bedchamber. It was an island of serenity, decorated in the finest of eighteenth-century French furnishings. These included fine-crafted marquetry tables, some inlaid with brass, others with tortoise-shell. The chairs were covered with pale-blue damask. A 1720 Angel bed with the canopy attached to the wall was also draped in damask. The bed had been proudly presented to her on her eighteenth birthday by Lord Stewart, who had been enormously pleased with the idea.

The walls were painted panels with the most exquisite painted scenes of animals, flowers, and trees. The panels were ornemaniste trimmed in gold leaf. The pastel colors and the tall windows, which let in great shafts of light, all culminated in an ethereal, feminine elegance. It suited her niece to perfection.

Angel turned. "I was just thinking about this evening. It is my first grand ball and I hope it proves more successful than some of the small gatherings we've attended."

"I know, my dear, but you must now think of resting. The Leightons are known for the extravagance of their entertainments. And we do want to look our best," Mary Beth coaxed in her best maiden-aunt voice. "I think you should take a rest. I know I have to, although I shan't need the energy you will to dance the night away. Ah, the pleasures

of spinsterhood. How lightly they are disregarded,"
she said with a little laugh.

The small gatherings they had previously attended had been ordeals. The cool reception of the
matrons of the *ton*, who had danced in their
younger days in the company of Angel's dazzling
mother, had made those evenings dreadful.

"You lacked no attention from the gentlemen.
They practically fell over one another, vying for
your notice," Mary Beth reminded her.

"Tonight, surely I'll be less noted among the
throng of guests bound to attend," Angel said.
"Those frowning pious matrons with their . . . I hate
them!"

Mary Beth arched an eyebrow. Angel attributed
far too much of the cool reception as directed from
her mother's reputation. It was an excuse, skillfully used by those who saw in the engaging Lady
Harlan a threat to the success of their own
daughters. Unfortunately, this idea never occurred
to Angel; therefore, some of her discomfort was
unwarranted.

"My dear, they always have their say. With me,
it was a sickening pity. 'Poor Mary Beth Stewart
can't catch a husband.' Pay no mind to them.
They're worried sick you'll outshine their insipid
daughters."

Angel laughed. "With reason! I mean to do just
that. The fine line of attracting possible suitors and
not appear *too* charming, lest I'm compared to
Mother, is harrowing no matter how you look at it."

"You're right, of course." Mary Beth studied her
niece. She would always attract the opposite sex.
Her fair, delicate air and unique blue eyes under
generously, fringed lashes beckoned young men, as
easily as the Lorelei of the Rhine. Desire to protect

the seemingly fragile beauty leapt in the heart of several young men who imagined their roles somewhere between Sir Galahad and Saint George, the dragon slayer.

Mary Beth knew that behind the dainty appearance lay the heart of a lion. Though inclined to be impetuous, her niece made serious efforts to control that aspect of her nature. Above all else, she had a strength far beyond her years, which stemmed from having to justify herself as separate from her mother.

Angel's strength showed in a confidence she purposely tried to convey. Mary Beth knew this fortitude was contrary to Angel's delicate appearance, but men are known to see what they wish to see, and too often that is only the surface. She was adorable, a pocket Venus. And a rich one.

"Angel, you must simply ignore those tabbies. You'll be a great success. You have yet to face the patronesses of Almack's. You will need all your acting skills," Mary Beth said, leveling a knowing look.

A seraphic smile lit Angel's face, and a devilish gleam lit her eyes. "I think, perhaps, I should choose to remain single. Who needs a husband to tell one what to do?"

Mary Beth smiled. "You know my father's wishes on that, dear. He will see you wed."

"To some penurious popinjay, and I vow it will not be so. Have you looked over the gentlemen in the marriage mart? No wonder you stayed single," Angel teased.

"My dear, they all aren't fools, though I must admit outstanding gentlemen are rather scarce, to say the least."

Angel looked at the neat, trim figure of her aunt. She gave an aura of propriety with her serene face and modest dress. There was an appealing quality about her, and Angel wondered why she hadn't married, but dared not ask.

"What of our host this evening, the Marquess of Kendall?" Angel asked with a twinkle in her eye.

"Lord Leighton is marvelously attractive. He looks like something Michaelangelo might have created. A bit risqué, I'm told, but *very* pleasant to look upon. And 'look upon' is all your grandfather would allow, I'm sure," Mary Beth confided.

"Ah, but now you have whetted my appetite. I shall view this paragon with interest."

"You don't need a handsome rake. You need propriety, and believe me, Lord Leighton is a well-known lady's man!

"How very interesting! Does he have kept women?" Angel asked.

"Angel, you devil! How can you speak so? Where in heaven's name did you learn that? You'll be the death of me!" Mary Beth looked as if she were about to faint.

"I learned about kept women at Witherspoon's Seminary for Young Ladies, though not in the class-room, of course. Don't take on so. I was just teasing. You brought up the subject. I shall not disappoint you in my behavior, I assure you."

"I know dear, it's—"

"I know, I know—Mother, God rest her soul."

Mary Beth rolled her eyes to heaven and sighed.

"Can we just take a peek at this god-man?" Angel answered half in jest, simply not able to resist the last shot.

"Indeed, we both shall," Mary Beth whispered, "but very discreetly, to be sure."

2

Ward Leighton, Marquess of Kendall, could be described in one word: captivating. People basked in the charm of his company. He left a trail of smiles in his wake. It was not as if he were jovial, for he was not. He simply made people feel good. It was as if he were interested in only you. For that moment, you were the most interesting or fascinating person he could choose to be with. This, of course, explains his success with women. For every true connoisseur of women knows, few can resist being utterly engaging.

This singular charm made most feminine defenses easy to breach. To his credit, if such can be so credited, he avoided virgin ladies and all young women seeking a permanent connection. He preferred the sophisticated charmer. His conquests were well aware of the direction their acquaintance would take and followed with delicious anticipation, seldom finding disappointment.

He now struggled over his neckcloth, softly swearing at the near impossibility of creating the perfect folds it sported less than two hours ago.

A little laugh escaped Lady Wharton's full lips,

slightly swollen from the passionate kisses Ward had given her. She tied the Chinese silk robe about her narrow waist, thinking she would miss him terribly. He was a kind and satisfying lover.

"I shall miss you," she sighed.

He caught her reflection and their eyes met. "I doubt for long. You are not a lady to be without a cicisbeo worshiping at your feet."

She laughed. "Perhaps, but I shall be back from Scotland by fall. How I hate Castle Calvine. It's really quite dreary, but Alister insists. It is necessary that I accommodate him," she said, her brown eyes soft and luminous.

"Since he is so accommodating toward you, I suspect," Leighton replied.

She crooked an eyebrow at the veiled rancor. "He totally understands and cares not one wit. After all, Ward, he is over sixty." She fluffed her raven curls around her shoulders and came to slip her arms around his waist. "Truly, I shall miss you."

Ward turned and dropped a light kiss on the tip of her dainty nose. "And so shall I miss you, pet."

She laughed again, "I'll not find another so well . . . so . . ."

"Accommodating?" he asked.

"Don't be churlish, Ward. We both knew it could not last. Perhaps, when I return, if you have not found a new love . . ." Her words trailed away as she looked into his eyes. No, she thought, it is over for him also.

Ward picked up his blue superfine cloth jacket. "You'll have to play the valet, my dear."

She helped him into the close-fitting coat and once more admired his fine shoulders, which needed no padding. He must be a tailor's dream as well as a lady's, she thought with a pretty smile.

He lifted her chin with his slender fingers and

looked at her a moment. "It's been a pleasure to be in your company. Good luck to you in Scotland. I'm sure you'll find a rugged Scotsman to while away your afternoons, my pet."

"You'll not be long without company either, I'll wager. You should think of marriage and begin your nursery, Ward. You're not getting any younger."

"You sound like my mother. My god, it is time for us to part. We're both not getting any younger, pet," he teased.

"Ward, you beast! What a thing to say to a lady," she said, sticking her tongue out at him.

He pulled her to him for the last time and kissed her thoroughly. "That might make the Scots less appealing."

"Men are conceited fools. You're no less than the rest."

Ward laughed as he placed his hat upon his head and picked up his walking stick. "Good-bye, I'll see my way out. I know it well enough," he said as he quietly left the room.

She stood a moment with her arms wrapped in a hug to her body to dispel the feeling of loss. She would miss Ward Leighton and was already mildly jealous of the next lucky lady.

Lady Wharton called her maid to ready her bath. There was the packing . . . so much to do before she left for the wilds of Scotland. Ward Leighton slipped from her thoughts as easily as he had slipped from her life.

The diversion of the afternoon with Lady Wharton had been an escape from the frantic activities of the preparations for the grand ball his mother was holding. The house was bedlam, with florists, caterers, maids, and footmen scurrying about in endless haste.

Turning his steps to Leighton Place, he smiled as he thought of his mother, but his smile quickly faded as a response of boredom overwhelmed him. He wondered what he was looking for. The void he carried was vague and yet all-pervading.

Tonight, at least, would keep him occupied. Thinking of his mother, he wondered just how much of a disappointment he was to her. She was unique, witty, and forthright, characteristics he admired and seldom found among the simpering ladies of the *ton*. Perhaps, he thought, it is time for me to look elsewhere. Still, he could not imagine himself married. He had never been able to fix his attentions on any one lady because he had simply never found one with enough intellectual depth to hold him.

He knew why: he was a cynic. He expected little from women except shallowness, and that is exactly what he had always found. Perhaps he found only what he anticipated, he wasn't sure. He shrugged. Well, he must do his duty to his mother. He would play the interested host and carefully extend his attentions over many ladies so that no mamas could attribute a compliment as a prelude to matrimony.

Lady Angel, Lady Mary Beth, and Lord Stewart entered the beautiful ballroom as their names were announced.

Lord Leighton stood with his mother, receiving each guest. Judging by the numbers in attendance, Angel wondered how they could still seem so enthusiastic in each greeting.

Angel wore a white muslin gown of the simplest lines. The square neck was beaded in tiny seed pearls, as were the gathered, short sleeves. The slender column of skirt ended in a train. Her pale hair was caught up in a silver filigree band enriched with pearls. A pale India shawl of blues and rose offered a rich contrast to the purity of the white of her costume. Few ladies wore any color but white, although there were a few pastels seen and some darker shades worn by older matrons who clung to earlier fashion.

Lord Leighton watched the Marquess of Farnham and the lovely lady on his arm approach. She was tiny, with glowing alabaster skin and pale flaxen hair. Her curls tumbled down her shoulders in artful disarray.

"Good evening, Anton. How delighted I am to see you," Lady Leighton said, extending her hand to Lord Stewart.

"You know my daughter, Mary Beth, but have you met my granddaughter, Lady Angel Harlan?" he replied, bowing over Lady Leighton's hand.

"Good evening, Lady Stewart. How kind of you to join us. I see you will have the pleasure of presenting your charming niece. What a lovely child." Lady Leighton turned to Angel. "We are honored to have you join us this evening. You are to make your come-out, I understand," she said, sending a warm, welcoming smile.

Angel responded to the warmth immediately with a merry smile as she made her curtsy. "Yes, and I do hope you will attend my ball. You are most kind to invite me this evening." Angel's voice faltered a second, for she had thus far received too many cool receptions, and Lady Leighton's graciousness pleased her profoundly.

"Nonsense, you are an enchanting young lady and shall certainly add grace to this evening's entertainment. May I present my son, the Marquess of Kendall, Lord Ward Leighton?"

Ward had been studying the exquisite face of the young lady before him. He was intrigued by the pale skin and silver-gold hair, but it was her unique eyes that ignited a reaction that traveled through his body.

They were navy rimmed irises surrounded by an almost-pale-cream center. He had never seen such brilliant eyes, more like beacons dominating her oval face. The open, frank appraisal emanating from them was unmistakable. He could not tell what they said, but knew he was being measured, even if only for the split second she gazed at him. She lowered her eyes and dipped in a slight curtsy.

A tremor passed through his body. He was surprised at his curiosity on just what that evaluation was. Bowing, he took her hand to his lips. "I am delighted to make your acquaintance. As host to this evening's entertainment, I hope to claim a dance later."

"But of course," she softly replied, then moved with her grandfather and Mary Beth into the ballroom.

"What a striking girl," he whispered to his mother as they turned to greet the other guests.

Lady Leighton cast a swift glance at her attractive son and tried to discern if the remark was only a mild observation or one that denoted interest. The latter thought leapt as a hope in her breast, and she decided to pursue that possibility.

"Actually, I thought her quite the most out-standing young lady. Rather breathtaking I should say," she whispered. Then she extended her greeting to the next guest.

Ward chuckled. Lady Leighton smiled, she knew he was reading her matchmaking mind.

Angel restrained herself from the overwhelming

desire to turn around and look once more upon the face of Lord Leighton. He was the most compelling man she had ever seen. He was handsome, yes, but it was not that. There were other handsome men. He radiated a glow as warm as the sun. Her skin tingled from that radiance.

"Tell me about Lord Leighton, Grandfather," she asked.

Lord Stewart turned to look at Angel. "Ah, there's a dangerous man. He's known to have a devastating effect on all the ladies. Take warning, child, he avoids the marriage mart with the passion that angels avoid hell, and so should my Angel," he said, squeezing her hand, which rested on his arm.

She turned to her aunt, who looked right into her eyes, as if to say, "I told you so." They both smiled with decided approval.

The evening was splendid. Angel had no time to notice any slights, for she was surrounded by gentlemen of every age and bent. Dancing every dance, she blossomed with the lighthearted banter and effusive compliments. A cynical twinkle sparkled in her eyes; no doubt, Grandfather had conveniently revealed the size of her dowry. Among her devotees were a considerable number of rather impoverished aristocrats. She was more than amused at the gracious response of their mothers.

Choosing a husband may be more diverting than I ever imagined, she thought with a derisive gleam in her eyes.

It was at this very moment that she looked up into the face of the Marquess of Kendall. He noted the provocative expression in her outstanding eyes and returned an intimate smile. Angel's eyebrow arched in suspicion.

The disarming smile broadened. "I believe this

is the set that you have so graciously consented to me," he said, offering his hand as if the matter was settled.

"I am not certain, sir, if this is the one you claimed," she said.

He raised an eyebrow and softly laughed. "Don't count me among those swooning swains, Lady Harlan. I promise not to bore you with hollow compliments. You might find that in itself refreshing."

"Indeed," Angel replied, placing her hand in his and feeling a sudden sense of affinity. She glanced up at his handsome profile and he turned to look at her.

She considered his face a moment and realized there was a hidden quality beneath the formal manners he graciously displayed. This, of course, could be said about anyone in the room, including herself, but it was as though she read something else. How odd, she thought. Her other partners evoked no such sensation.

The patterned steps of the dance gave them little time to speak other than the briefest of comments. He moved with the grace of an accomplished dancer and Angel's own concentration on the steps revealed the novice of her ballroom experience.

Cordially thanking her, Lord Leighton escorted her to the side of her grandfather, bowed, and took his leave.

Snapping open her lovely fan, Angel fanned her glowing cheeks while her grandfather remarked on the rather notorious Lord Leighton.

"A fine figure of a man, I'd say. Beware, if those are blushes you are attempting to fan away," he warned in a half-teasing, half-serious manner. He lifted his bushy eyebrows as he made his point.

Angel, of course, recognized this facial quirk and

put her fan into agitated motion. "Grandfather, please keep in mind I am not interested in every man I dance with. This room is oppressive with the heat and I've danced every set. No wonder my cheeks are flushed! You needn't warn me at every turn. I assure you I shall have more sense than that," she replied in obvious pique.

Before he could answer her annoyed retort, she was whisked away by yet another young blade. He watched as she laughingly joined the forming set for some country dances.

Lord Stewart beamed with pride. His grand-daughter was doing quite well for herself this evening. He'd have her safely married in no time at all. A satisfied expression remained upon his face the entire evening.

Angel's feet were protesting to the evening's frantic activity, since they were ensconced in only soft, heelless dancing slippers tied with satin ribbons. It was a relief to take her place at the table with several young couples following the dinner dance.

The dining room was arranged with dozens of small round tables to accommodate four to six people. This was to give chances of intimate con-versation to the guests. There were many daughters and sons to marry off, and such arrangements were often used to facilitate getting to know one another under the watchful eyes of parents.

The table covers were pink and dropped to the floor. On each table sat a small bouquet of pink and white roses giving a springlike atmosphere and delicate scent. The room was charming, and light-hearted laughter and conversation mingled with the sound of tinkling glasses.

She was being escorted by Lord John Hatton, second son of the Earl of Bath. He was tall and thin

with a shy smile and soft voice. Obviously smitten
by the beauty he sat next to, he never took his eyes
from her face and never opened his mouth. She was
grateful for Lord Smedley, who was a bit of a wag,
and his fiancée, Miss Mathews, who giggled at his
every sally. They allowed Angel and her reticent
partner no awkward moments of embarrassed
silence.

Smiling, she sat. She could think of nothing but
her aching feet, and she wiggled her toes to relieve
the pain. Since the table covers on the small round
tables reached the floor, Angel made a terrible
mistake. She quietly reached down and slipped off
her right slipper. Crossing her leg, she reached and
rubbed the aching foot.

Ah, she thought, that felt so good. She was
positive she would never walk again or at least
would be in bed a week while her feet healed.
Sitting up, she reached for her shoe with her foot
but it wasn't there. She gently felt around with her
toes. No shoe.

The pasted smile began to fade. She bumped Lord
Smedley's leg with her searching toes and he
stopped his conversation in midsentence.

Angel blushed to the roots of her pale silver-gold
hair. Smedley launched on, wondering if Lady
Harlan was signaling an inappropriate interest. The
idea filled his masculine ego with delight. He
reached and patted Miss Mathews' hand, while
thinking not everyone could be as fortunate as his
fiancée in their choice of husband.

Angel, of course, had no such thought and began
to panic over the whereabouts of her shoe. I must
stay calm, she told herself. Ah, the very thing. She
dropped her fan and reached to retrieve it in hopes
of taking a quick peek under the table.

Lord Hatton, God bless his mother's teaching,

quickly reached to do the heroic honor himself. They bumped heads and Angel saw stars for a moment. Stunned, she sat back. Lord Hatton, profusely apologizing for colliding into her, gallantly returned the fan.

"Thank you," she feebly replied.

As luck would have it, the wayward shoe had traveled under Lord Hatton's chair and the slender ribbon trailed out onto the floor. Just then Sir Dudley-Welton, of prodigious size and heavy-footed step, lumbered on his way again to the food-ladened table. The heel of his shoe caught the ribbon and he proceeded with the tiny white satin slipper trailing behind.

Angel's eyes flew open. A gasp escaped her mouth as she placed her fan over it. She squeezed her eyes shut a moment, thinking, Now, what?

"Are you ill, Lady Harlan?" her up-to-now-silent partner asked.

"No," she whispered, trying not to stare at the disappearing shoe. She raised her horrified eyes and met those of Lord Leighton, who was seated nearly halfway across the room. She stared in disbelief and her once-flushed cheeks drained white. She slowly moved her fan from her lips and delicately pointed to the trailing slipper, which was now bouncing rather merrily in pursuit of Sir Dudley-Welton.

Lord Leighton looked down and espied the shoe, then glanced up in question. Angel nodded and rolled her eyes to heaven in search of deliverance. A smile appeared on his lips and he nodded. Deftly reaching out his foot, he caught the wayward shoe and drew it in.

Sir Dudley-Welton, unaware of his trailing companion, went blissfully forward in direct pursuit of those delicious little lobster patties.

Leighton retrieved the slipper, tucked in the ribbons, and placed it under his coat. Make no mistake, this was no mean feat! It had taken his valet fifteen minutes to get his lordship into the "perfect work of art by Shultz." The bulge was slightly discernible and Lord Leighton sent a speaking wink toward Lady Angel as he rose from his table.

I could die right here and now. Lord, let me perish from the face of the earth, Angel thought with a pounding heart. Then the humor of the situation melted her chagrin and a trembling smile turned the corners of her lips.

Leighton excused himself from the guests with whom he had been seated, and sauntered to Lady Harlan's table.

"Lady Harlan, my mother has requested me to fetch you. She has asked me to escort you to her, if that is agreeable," he said, and light from his blue-green eyes shone in devilish delight.

Angel rose, adjusting her train to cover her right foot. She almost tripped on it as she took Lord Leighton's arm. He reached his hand to steady her and she could feel it burning her arm. She glanced up at him and found a sweet smile and understanding expression. Her body relaxed under such kindness as she accompanied him out of the dining room.

The marble hall was cool and soothing to her foot, and she couldn't repress a tenuous giggle.

"I am extremely embarrassed, but thank you for rescuing me," she said.

"Ah, but we have to replace the shoe. Now, where shall we do that without ending up in some dark corner? With your apparent luck the Archbishop of Canterbury would come upon us. Now, let's see," he said.

He guided her to the gallery, which housed a fine collection of art. A few guests were wandering about, observing the paintings and paying no mind to those entering or leaving.

Angel self-consciously sat on a delicate gold *fauteuil*. The marquess removed the slipper from his coat and knelt before her. He took her foot and placed the shoe on it and tied the ribbons. A shiver ran through her, for never had she been in such an intimate situation.

Leighton briskly stood up and stretched out his hand. "Now, I shall return you to your grandfather. It would not do well for you to be too long in my company," he said. The veiled rancor in his voice was not lost on Angel's ears.

"You have done me a great kindness. Can you imagine the clucking of the hens if I had to chase after my shoe? Believe me, I have enough notoriety without adding total lack of breeding to it," she said, and the vision of actually chasing after her shoe brought a spirited giggle. She turned her brilliant smile to him.

"With such a reward you may consider me always at your service," he said, looking into her eyes and returning an equally enchanting smile. "Not all things lost can so easily be recovered."

Angel searched his smiling eyes with their crinkled corners and saw an expression she did not understand any more than she understood his remark.

3

Helmsley, the butler, a tall spare man who had been in Lord Stewart's service forty years, shook his head in dismay at the confusing activity centered in the entrance hall. He had been besieged by a host of young men calling to see if Lady Harlan survived the strenuous evening of dancing. Helmsley sniffed at that ridiculous remark, for Lady Harlan could survive a dozen such evenings and be ready to ride in the morning.

Notes and flowers arrived in such a profusion, he had just time to delegate their placement before the arrival of yet another offering to Lady Angel's charm. He vowed that if there was no letup, he was bound to order a lord of the realm placed on a table and announce the arrival of a bouquet. His eyes danced with the thought as he again answered an impatient knock on the door.

Opening the door, Helmsley rolled his eyes to heaven when astounded by the largest bouquet of yellow roses he had ever beheld. So large, in fact, he could see only the legs of the bearer of this munificent offering.

"Allow me, sir," Helmsley said, taking the

monumental spray. He was astounded to find Lord
Hatton standing as the proud bearer, since
bouquets were seldom hand-delivered by a suitor.

"Is Lady Harlan in and receiving guests?" Lord
Hatton stuttered from a mouth in a beet-red face.

"Yes, my lord. Allow me to escort you to the blue
salon," Helmsley said, handing the bouquet to an
anxious footman. The footman had seen the precar-
ious arrangement swaying and grabbed for it just
as Helmsley was about to lose control.

No young man, Helmsley captiously shook his
head at all this nonsense. Great heavens, he thought,
how peaceful it had been before Lady Angel's home-
coming! But fortunately by the looks of things,
she'll soon be claimed, and life would return to tran-
quil days. These thoughts changed no expression on
his stoic, lined face.

The blue salon was cluttered with an astounding
variety of admiring men, all vying for Angel's
attention. She stood in the center of the gathering,
responding in light repartee, which one would
assume was vastly amusing, based on the reaction
of her delighted audience.

Lord Hatton first frowned at the assembly, then
burst into a broad grin for the young lady standing
in the middle of the group.

"How kind of you to call," she greeted him,
graciously extending her hand. Her eyes could have
easily been said to match the flower arrangement
in size, since her amazement was no less then
Helmsley's.

"Lord Hatton, never have I seen such a beautiful
bouquet," she said, overwhelmed by the size, as the
footman placed Lord Hatton's offering on the piano.
Her hand fluttered to her lips to hide a smile, only
to give a delicate, helpless air that Lord Hatton immediately wished to protect, forever.

He admired her beauty with a pounding heart. If he could only write an ode to her charms, in the manner of Byron, to be sure. "An Ode to a Fragile Beauty," Lord Hatton thought, flushing with love-sick emotion.

"Just a little expression of my regard," he said, bringing himself out of his reverie and bowing over her slender white hand.

That was the longest string of words she had heard him utter, and she smiled. "I am flattered, for never have I seen anything so magnificent."

Observing the little drama, Aunt Mary Beth surveyed the yellow fragrant mass and clicked her tongue between her teeth. She sent an appraising glance at the thin quiet man. Now, there's one who is not what he seems to be. Pure defiance bought that bouquet. Old man Hatton would consider it a foolish waste of money. This observation amused her, for she was an ardent student of human nature.

An ebullient Angel glowed with the flattering attention, but beamed even more when the last suitor had departed.

Her modest demeanor disappeared as she threw up her arms. "Never in my life! Can you explain it?"

"Your charm, of course," Aunt Mary Beth replied in mock seriousness.

"No, it's the size of my dowry."

"Lord Hatton doesn't need any, although he is a second son. I knew his father in my younger days. Never spent a groat he didn't have to. Young Hatton is apparently a very independent man. Does exactly as he pleases," Aunt Mary Beth remarked.

"You can't be serious. I never met anyone so willowy. Why, one could bend him around one's finger."

"My, my, my, know everything, do you? And so quickly! Your astuteness is enviable. Chaperoning

you during your Season promises to be very entertaining. I tell you: Lord Hatton doesn't do a thing
he doesn't wish to. I'll even wager he manages to
have things his way," Aunt Mary Beth challenged.

"You're serious," Angel said, shaking her pale
curls in disbelief.

"I am. Mark my words, all things aren't as they
seem. Especially people. Watch them, you'll see
what I mean," Aunt Mary Beth insisted.

Angel laughed.

Aunt Mary Beth smiled benignly. Well, I'm just
a spinster, and few credit me with profound
wisdom. I'll watch this tale unfold and crow later,
she thought.

"By the by, this bouquet came while you were
basking in all that heady attention. Have you seen
it? I think not, for the card remains unopened."

Angel looked down at the tiny white porcelain
slipper filled with violets. A quiver ran down her
spine. She reached over and gently touched it. Her
eyes caught Mary Beth's intense gaze, and she
turned away to hide her expression while opening
the card.

Written in a clean masculine stroke were the
words: "My compliments to the newest reigning
belle. Please consider me at your service anytime
in the future. WL."

Angel's blue eyes glowed and a fleeting smile
turned the corners of her mouth. A rosy hue
reached her cheeks.

"Who sent the charming gift?" Aunt Mary Beth
asked in seeming innocence.

"Lord Leighton."

"Indeed?"

Taking up the little china slipper, Angel touched
the petals and slowly left the room.

"Indeed," Mary Beth said again, aloud but to herself.

If Lord Leighton's unfathomable gaze the night he saved her from embarrassment, or his gift, lingered in Angel's mind, she had little time to contemplate them.

"We are to call on Lady Jersey, and I want you on your best behavior," Mary Beth said, slipping on her lavender kid gloves.

"You do not have to warn me. I shall be the model of modest decorum," Angel replied, giving a final appraisal to her appearance in the pier mirror before they passed through the front door.

"The weather is so promising: it must be an omen for my acceptance at Almack's" Angel said.

Mary Beth laughed. "You're correct. I have the feeling that we're about to embark on the most remarkable adventure."

"What do you mean?" Angel asked, feeling the excitement, as if something wonderful would happen.

Lady Stewart and Lady Angel Harlan were ushered into the presence of the elegant Lady Jersey. The patroness of Almack's appraised the demure and delicate, pale-blond, young lady. Nothing like her flamboyant mother, she observed with a sigh of relief. She had practically been coerced by Lord Stewart to accept his granddaughter into the select halls of Almack's. The child had the family background and, from her first observation, the necessary poise.

"My dear Lady Harlan, how are you enjoying the first entertainments of the Season?" Lady Jersey asked.

"I must admit it is rather exciting and somewhat

overwhelming; however, the parties I have attended have been very enjoyable."

"I hear much praise on your beauty and modest manners. You are bound to be a success," Lady Jersey said, wondering how the child would handle so lavish a compliment.

"If that is what you have heard, then I shall take it that you have been speaking with my grandfather. His view of the matter is decidedly partial," Angel said with a dimpled smile.

Lady Jersey narrowed her eyes. The child is clever.

"Your come-out ball is to be held in two weeks. Then there is the court presentation. I imagine you are nervous over the attention you must face," Lady Jersey said.

"Well, yes, it is rather daunting. I have Aunt Mary Beth at my side, and people have been most kind in helping me find my way," Angel replied, resting her gaze on her interrogator.

Lady Jersey smiled. The child lies, she has been snubbed on more than one occasion. I like her spunk, clothed in demure calmness.

"My dear, we welcome you. I shall have your vouchers sent to you. You will be a charming addition to this Season. May I take the opportunity to wish you much success? If I can be of any assistance to you, please let me know. There are some obstacles, to be sure, but somehow I am convinced you will easily handle any small hazards."

"You are kind. Thank you for your support. I hope to fulfill Grandfather's wishes," Angel said, dropping her eyes.

Lady Jersey smiled, rose, and bade them good day. She watched the diminutive young lady leave the room. There was a power about her. Lady Jersey

could not define it, but she knew, without doubt,
this young lady could never be convinced to run off.
It was amusing to be an arbiter of fashion. One was
able to participate in intriguing circumstances of
human interest and folly. If I am not mistaken, Lady
Harlan will do very well for herself. Such demure
modesty is bound to attract, but there was also the
direct gaze of her brilliant eyes . . . Interesting,
Lady Jersey thought.

Angel was besieged with invitations to parties,
balls, and routs. Swept up in the fashionable whirl,
she met more people than she could remember, and
some she wished to forget. While a cluster of beaux
trailed in tow, she appeared to give no one suitor
favored attention. Treating most of them with a
light, teasing flirtation, she deftly kept them at
arm's length.

The Duke of Albrion, Earl of Seaton, William
Augustus Corners, stood engaged in a conversation
with several gentlemen awaiting the pleasure of
Lady Burney's musicale. Tonight she was offering
dancing to the music of an imported Viennese
orchestra. The lady considered herself a patron of
the arts and managed to attract the best musicians.
The duke seldom missed her gatherings. Since he
was immensely popular and highly regarded by his
peers, his presence was considered an honor to any
presiding hostess. The fact that he was considered
the most eligible bachelor only added to his
consequence.

He was tall and carried his height with natural,
athletic grace. Strikingly handsome, he radiated an
assurance of his attractiveness and lofty titles.
Never, as a gentleman, did he display arrogance
and, therefore, was known for his chivalrous
manners. Among his attributes were dark-brown

wavy hair with hints of auburn, soft expressive
brown eyes, and classic features. His broad
shoulders fitted a superbly tailored rust velvet coat.
The plain waistcoat and carefully tied neckcloth
proclaimed him no dandy. He sported a large
diamond pin and gold signet ring. By any dandy's
standard, he was modestly dressed. On him, it was
nothing short of spectacular. If he was aware of his
attractiveness, it was not discernible.

His keen brown eyes caught sight of Angel as she
entered the room with Aunt Mary Beth and Lord
Stewart. He was acquainted with Stewart and
wondered how the young lady was connected to
him. He remembered seeing her at several large
balls but had not been introduced. Observing her
grace of movement and animated smile, he decided
that an introduction would be imminent.

"Who is the beauty in the chiffon dress with the
blue ribbons," Lord Corners drawled.

"Which one? They all wear white dresses with
blue ribbons," Lord Rutherford said.

"The one entering with Lord Stewart."

"Ah, that's his granddaughter. He dotes on the
chit. She's just come up to London, about to have
her come-out ball. Rather famous mother, if you're
up on your gossip. Ran away with some Italian
count. The scandal killed her father, Lord Chester
Harlan. Understand Stewart's put twenty thousand
pounds on her. Every fortune hunter in the realm
is bound to woo her."

"She has grace and beauty; I doubt she needs
such a dowry," Corners added with a hint of
reproof. He did not deal in common gossip.

"Well, the scandal of her mother makes one
wonder if she's as impulsive. Rather intriguing, I
should say."

"You say too much, Rutherford. Lord Stewart may be a daring investor, but he's a high stickler. I should imagine she's been carefully under his eyes."

"Aye, your grace, so it seems. She appears to be rather circumspect. Doesn't cater to any of her many admirers," Rutherford answered, attempting to recover lost ground.

"I should think, Rutherford, you would refrain from common gossip about the young lady's mother. A gentleman would not indulge in such talk," Corners said.

"Sorry, old man. Didn't know you had an interest."

"I've never met the lady. How could I have an interest? I would refrain from censuring her for some foolish actions of her mother's. Introduce her to me," he commanded.

Following Lord Rutherford, the Duke of Albrion crossed the large room to Lord Stewart's side. Angel looked into the face of the most handsome man she had ever seen. His warm eyes lingered on her as the introduction was made. She had heard of the Earl of Albrion, in the most glowing terms.

The great duke took her hand and raised it to his lips as he executed an elegant bow. Mary Beth turned positively girlish with a giggle, and even blushed when Lord Corners acknowledged her with a flattering comment about one other occasion when he had previously met her.

"I do declare, how could you possibly remember that occasion, your grace?" she said, her usual serenity disappearing in a little twitter.

"I never forget a pretty face," he softly replied.

Aunt Mary Beth Stewart fell solidly into his pocket. Amazed, Angel smiled, then glanced slightly askance at so pretty a speech. A charmer, another ladies' man. Great heavens, they're as common as false compliments, she thought.

"Would you honor me by being my partner in the next set, Lady Harlan?" the duke asked with a deep resonant voice.

"I've already claimed that dance," Lord Hatton piped up in a squeaky voice. He had witnessed the introduction with a sinking heart. How did one compete with the great Duke of Albrion? His knees trembled along with his voice.

"Indeed? I'm sure you'd not be so churlish as to deny me that pleasure, for if I am correct in my estimate, you have claimed several."

"Well, yes, but . . ." Hatton faltered and all was lost. As the duke had calculated, Lord Stewart took the situation in hand.

"Do run along, Hatton, you can have your next claim for a dance," Lord Stewart said with a wave of his stubby fingers.

Angel stood, bemused. Her managing grandfather had quickly settled the matter, and there was nothing to do but take the proffered arm of the Duke of Albrion. She smiled at her grandfather's promise of a husband of her own choosing. He'd see her pushed in whatever direction he chose. Only he wasn't aware just how stubborn her feet would be when pushed in any direction. A defiant sparkle flickered a second in her eyes.

The duke was watching her as he escorted her to the assembling set, and he became immediately intrigued by the mystery the expression imparted.

"At risk of repeating what I am sure you have answered so many times, are you enjoying the Season?" he asked, to draw her into conversation, however mundane.

"Very much so. It is most exciting but I fear I do

miss the country," Angel replied, for she had spent little time at Harlan Hall in recent years. At the moment it was the truth. All these entertainments were beginning to wear thin.

"What an enchanting idea. I couldn't agree more! I long for the heather-scented moorland of Yorkshire, and while I enjoy a visit to London, I am always glad to return to Castle Newbray. You must see it sometime."

She noted the sincerity in his voice and glanced up at him just as they parted in the moving pattern of the dance steps. His warm brown eyes glowed with kindness. She was immediately taken by this aspect far more than by his handsome appearance. Her opinion of him changed. What it had been before, she could not have put into words, but it had something to do with the fact that she did not trust handsome men. They were usually far too full of themselves. She would never join an adoring throng to some fair face with a vacant, self-centered mind.

Angel noted more than a few appreciative glances aimed toward her partner and no fewer frowns directed at her. My, my, the mamas are worried I'll charm Lord Corners, she thought, and devilishly sent a beguiling, appreciative glance of her own. The duke smiled in return.

She decided then and there that this might all be more entertaining than ever expected, and a wicked light glowed in her brilliant eyes.

Lord Corners, who considered himself above the wiles of insipid ladies, felt a constriction in his chest. The child is enchanting, he decided. And when the great Duke of Albrion decided something, it was so.

"Perhaps I can get up a party to go down to Hampton Court for an afternoon's outing. Now, that might just be the thing for our country

longings. Would that please you?" he asked, amazed
at his impetuousness. Suddenly, he felt like a
salmon caught easily on a fly line in a Sottish firth.
He stiffened and a closed expression crossed his
face.

Angel noticed his change of expression and a
giggle bubbled silently inside her. "Why, I should
like that above all else. It would be a delight to
escape stuffy rooms," she exclaimed a little too
enthusiastically.

A flicker crossed his eyes. A bit high-spirited,
perhaps, but that is easily cured. A failing of the
young, he wisely reasoned.

"I'll make arrangements. We must include Lady
Stewart, to be sure. I'll make the plans, and feel free
to include anyone you wish to have join us," he said.

The music ended and Lord Corners escorted her
to her waiting grandfather. "Thank you for the
pleasure of the dance. I shall call on you so we can
settle the plans for the outing. I look forward to
that," he said as he bowed and departed with a
feeling of total disbelief over his impulsive offer.

Angel stood transfixed. Mary Beth stood transfixed next to her.

"He's calling? What did he mean about an
outing?" Aunt Mary Beth whispered behind her fan.

"He's going to arrange an outing to Hampton
Court. You're invited and anyone else I might
choose. Imagine," Angel whispered back.

"We'll speak of this later," Mary Beth cautioned.

Angel nodded. He was interesting. Turning, she
looked up into the eyes of Lord Leighton, who stood
several feet away. His blue-green eyes lingered a
second. A start went through her body. She had not
seen him here. When did he arrive?

Leighton nodded to her in discreet greeting, then
turned to continue speaking with the beautiful

Duchess of Devonshire. Angel watched him a
moment. The warmth of his gaze seemed to reach
her and spread through her body. Aghast at her
reaction, she dropped her eyes and raised her chin
in an involuntary act of defiance.

"Lady Harlan, I now claim my dance," Lord
Hatton said.

"Why, of course," she replied. As she took to the
dance floor, she did not see Lord Leighton's eyes
follow her movements.

During the remaining evening Angel displayed a
cool hauteur that she had not previously shown.
This may have dismayed her suitors; it did not,
however, dampen their enthusiasm. An intriguing
aura of aloofness about her sprang into being this
evening. She was fragile, helpless, flirtatious in an
unattainable way. These attributes, added to a
beauty with money, could drive a man to distraction. If human nature was constant, her
following would soon be legion.

4

Dear Libby,

I have not written lately simply because there has not been a moment to do so. I am busy with a great variety of social functions. You can't imagine some of the ideas hostesses think up. In some ways, the Season is great fun.

Everyone is acting and everyone else knows it! It's absolutely amazing. They pretend to be delighted with seeing one another or exclaim on the beauty of another's gown. Yet it's plain as Prinny's paunch, they're positively pea-green with envy. It's like a play unfolding.

I continue in the demure, if ever so flirtatious role and am doing it rather convincingly. So, I enact a role too. I can almost hear your disbelieving scoff on the word "demure," but 'tis true. As far as flirtatious, we never had a chance to practice at Witherspoon's, unless you count the coachman, Timothy Evans, and all he ever did was blush and stammer. We could never be sure we were getting it right. I assure you, Libby, we were. It's actually very easy. One only has to smile sweetly and raise one's eyes rather soulfully, somewhat like a sick cow. The whole thing is quite foolish until one comes into contact with someone like the Marquess of Kendall. I should be afraid to attempt flirting with him! He would see right through me, and think how humiliating that would be! It is not a problem, since I rarely see him, and then only from a distance. I am reduced to elegant nods, or at least I hope they are elegant. One can never really be sure about that sort of thing.

Generally, things are good. Grandfather is pleased with my progress. I have been most proper. The paragons of virtue, otherwise known as the patronnesses of Almack's, have given me their approval. The interview was uncomfortable; Lady Jersey looked me over with the precision of a diamond merchant. Apparently not found wanting, I was given my vouchers.

I was a bit churlish about the whole affair, and Mary Beth gave me a well deserved set-down. I am suffering from all the scrutiny. I feel like an insect in a laboratory, though I realize I must keep these thoughts to myself.

So now I take up the standard to catch a husband in earnest. Up until now, I believe, I didn't believe, if you can understand what I mean. It's just that now, I know I have to choose a husband. I do not even want one, or at least, I am not sure.

My suitors, several younger sons, several old men, and many poor relations, make up the general entourage. However, Lord Corners, the Duke of Albrion, has taken a notice. He is to set up a day's outing. We shall see. He's terribly handsome. He has great address and sense of his lofty position. It sets him apart, somehow. I assume it is best to have a remote husband; they're surely not as bossy, or nosy. I must keep that in mind.

Lord Leighton sent flowers and nodded to me at

several functions, but then he rescued me from a stupid mistake I made. Libby, never, never, slip off your shoe when at a ball. They're impossible to find again. Or if you do, make sure Lord Leighton is at hand.

Now you're not believing my claim of modesty and genteel manners. I promise I am the model of perfection.

Write me soon, I will keep you informed on my progress to stand entrancingly still while I chase and catch a query.

Love,
Angel

Angel folded the letter, wishing Libby were with her. What fun they would have! She felt restless and dissatisfied. Still smarting from Mary Beth's set-down, she lowered her head and rested her chin in her arms.

Instead of mealymouthing around, she wanted to . . . Heaven's only knew what she wanted. Surely, it wasn't being examined by a host of hypocrites to see if she could fit into the world of social hypocrites. Angel frowned.

Poor Mary Beth, saddled with an ungrateful child, she thought. "Mulish" could best describe me, she thought, not a model of perfection, as she had boasted to Libby, but a pattern of a spoiled child.

"Darling, you were perfect," Mary Beth had said, drawing off her gloves upon their return from the visit to Lady Jersey.

Angel blushed remembering her reply: "I am most gratified that my behavior passed your approval, as well as that of the inquisitor, Lady Jersey. I am weak with gratitude." The rancor of her voice was all too evident.

"I understand your annoyance, Angel. But I

cannot change the dictates of society. If, in fact, you must do penance for your mother's grasp for happiness, do not press me with your childlike antics," Mary Beth had said with an annoyance seldom heard in her voice.

"I understand, Angel. It is demeaning, but, in fact, we all must toe the mark. There is only so much that I may do as a spinster. You would do well to wear it a bit more lightly, or you will blurt out some unforgivable remark in pique, then all will be lost," Mary Beth said with a sigh of resignation.

"It cannot be much of a pleasure to carry me about to see that I'm accepted for vouchers at Almack's or any other such thing," Angel said softly with a sting of remorse.

"Frankly, Angel, I would prefer to be back in the country. So let us smile and do what is needed without childish complaints. It'll be easier, I assure you. Now that you have your vouchers, we must look to your court presentation. And these invitations," she said, picking up the envelopes from the silver tray.

Angel felt positively foolish. Mary Beth was being a saint through this whole ridiculous routine, and here she stood complaining.

Well, she had been declared a charming young lady and given her sponsorship. She would proceed to secure a husband, however distasteful that proved to be.

"Ward, it's been positively ages since you've taken tea with me. You're usually off on some business or other. I cannot even remember if you take cream," Lady Leighton bantered. "Are you well?" Lady Leighton continued, eyes wide with feigned innocence. She knew that he was undoubtedly in perfect health. She also understood it probably wasn't to take tea with her but with a blue-eyed charmer that had brought him into her company. Having almost despaired of his settling down, she could not resist toying with him.

"Cream, please," Lord Leighton drawled as he watched his mother gracefully lift the silver pot. She was right, he thought, it has been too long since I've taken tea with her. He would rectify that.

Lounging back, he waited for her to obligingly discuss Lady Harlan, sure that she would be dying to do so. He knew her better than she knew herself, or so he thought.

Lady Leighton paused a moment to view her son from under veiled lashes. He was all that a mother could wish. He was handsome, strong, and honorable. A bit naughty, perhaps, but that could be corrected with the right wife.

She noted the impeccable dress in the fashionable blue superfine coat and buff-colored pantaloons that seemed, these days, to be the uniform of the younger set. His Hessians sported tassels and a sheen of blinding gloss. Brummell had decreed that champagne brought out the best shine, and obviously he was right. She smiled. Even Ward listened to Brummel's dictates, and it amused her, for he would vehemently deny it. If only he would listen to her dictates and settle down.

"What brings the sly smile to your lips, Mother? Surely you have some scheme in that pretty head of yours," he said, hoping to bring her out.

"I was just thinking what a fine-looking man you are and that your Hessians look very shiny," she said.

Ward arched an eyebrow in surprise, then glanced at his boots. "So, you comment on my presence and the condition of my boots. I had expected something else."

"What else?" she asked, lifting her slender hand in a questioning gesture. The diamonds of her rings sparkled with her movement.

"I'm not sure. You do have something in mind, I can tell," he insisted. He shifted uncomfortably, wondering if she were deliberately being obtuse.

A spark entered her lively green eyes. *He is interested! He wants me to invite Lady Harlan to some entertainment, one where he might spend more time with her than the one dance usually permitted without drawing undue attention.* Pondering whether to draw him out with the request or make it herself, she sipped her tea.

He looked positively miserable. *How delightful,* she thought. She would do the gracious thing and ease his discomfiture.

"Ward, I thought Lord Stewart's charming granddaughter to be quite the belle of the Season. Did you notice her?"

"Mother, I would have to be blind not to notice her, even though she is but a slip of a girl." He smiled as he spoke.

"Yes, such elegant manners. A gently bred young lady, and rather shy, I should think. Nothing like her mother, whose indiscretions must be a burden for her. I daresay she is quite intimidated by it all."

"I doubt it," Ward replied. He remembered the steady intense gaze she sent him. There was far more to that lady than simpering manners.

"Really? I should say she was rather retiring," Lady Leighton insisted.

"Hurmp" Ward muttered.

"Hurmp? What do you mean by that?"

"Mean what by what?" Ward asked.

"Your hurmp was not hurmp that means, 'I see,' but hurmp that means 'I don't believe you,' " Lady Leighton explained in all seriousness.

Ward stared at her in disbelief. He was actually sitting here discussing the semantic value of "hurmp." He was either besotted or ready for Bedlam. And the thought left him nonplussed and infinitely preferring Bedlam.

"Well, which did you mean?" his mother pressed.

"I think she is no Mild Miss. She has a thought or two in her head and does very well with the hand she has to play," he stated very precisely.

"My! I can see that you have taken careful note of the lady. She is lovely, and perhaps we could—" Lady Leighton began only to be interrupted by the butler entering the room.

"Your pardon, Lady Leighton, Major-General Duncan MacDougal has called to see you," Parker announced.

"Don't let him stand in the hall. Send him in," Ward said, rising from his chair.

Lady Leighton's hand went unconsciously to adjusting her lace cap. Major-General MacDougal was an outstanding gentleman and invariably brought out in any woman who still breathed a desire to appear at her best.

A robust man with a proud military bearing entered the room. Tanned by India's sun, he sported a marvelous sepoy mustache, which was a common practice among returning English soldiers for the fierce appearance it evoked. However, the good humor of Major-General MacDougal could not be subdued by a mere mustache.

"Duncan, it's good to see you! When did you return from that heathen land? I am impressed with your new rank of major-general," Ward said, shaking his hand in obvious delight.

"A fortnight, and it's good to be back! Ah, Lady Leighton, I find you in blooming health," Major-General MacDougal said, bending over her outstretched hand. A soft brogue still lingered in the corners of his speech.

"It's so good to see you home again. London is never the same without you. I do hope you intend to stay awhile. Have you been to Scotland yet?" she asked.

"Aye, been in Edinburgh to see me mum. She's still spry and peppery as ever," he said with a hearty chuckle. "I hope to be here for some time, but there's that nasty little Corsican stirring things up a bit. Don't know when or where, but mark my words, we'll have to put a halt to the upstart. For now, I am here and eager to join in some civilized entertainment."

"Tell us how things are in India?" Ward asked.

"Troublesome. Major-General Wellesley saved British interests with the victories at Assaye and Argaum and greatly reduced the powers of the Mahrattas who aimed to drive out the British. The East Indian Company, alarmed at the cost of war, forced Wellesley's resignation. He saved their damned necks and they forced him out. Boggles the mind, greedy little—"

"Tea or a spot of sherry?" Ward interrupted.

"Ah, a spot of sherry, if you please. Did miss it, you know." MacDougal blushed. "Been in the army too long, I daresay. My pardons for getting rather carried away, Lady Leighton. Bit rough around the edges. I'll need some taking in hand if I'm to fit in a civilized salon again."

"I might venture to say, you'll be a refreshing addition," the marchioness remarked.

"Major-General Wellesley soon learned that using spirits in the Indian climate does not sustain one's health. Drink is the cause of death for many a good British soldier under that relentless sun. Wellesley insisted on abstinence. Kept us fit and able to make

forced marches of forty and sixty miles. That
regimen spelled the difference between success or
failure."

"Can't say I know him," Ward said.

"Anglo-Irish aristocrat. Related to Charles and
John Wesley in some way or other. Though not a
religious man that one could notice. Odd if you
think of it. If Charles Wesley had taken his
inheritance, it would not have passed to the family
of Robert Colley Wellesley. There might not have
been a Methodist church.

"Major-General Wellesley has taken a seat in the
Parliament to defend his brother, Robert, who has
also been brought home from India and forced to
give up the governorship. The East India Company
is full of greedy fools; don't know when they're well-
served, to my way of thinking. But enough politics,
for surely we bore Lady Leighton," MacDougal said.

"Why, I find this all fascinating, but now we must
consider a small dinner party to welcome you back.
Don't you agree, Ward?" Lady Leighton said.

Ward brightened. "Let us set the day," he said
enthusiastically as he poured them another glass
of sherry.

"We must call in some old friends you might wish
to see. There are several newcomers to the scene
whom you might admire," she said slyly, glancing
toward Ward.

"If I know your mother, the small gathering will
become a crush."

"Now, that would not suit our purposes, would
it?" Lady Leighton said.

Ward returned a triumphant look. "No, we will
make an intimate evening so that Duncan can bask
in the company of old friends."

"And new," she added, ever so sweetly.

5

The Prince of Wales did not wear his forty-four years well. In his younger days he had been undeniably handsome, but now the excesses of his prodigal life were plainly displayed on his fat and florid face. His growing corpulence could no longer be disguised by his cumberland corset. Under delusion, the Prince considered himself to be of very royal figure. Still, he was not without charm, and could dazzle with elegance, affability, and warmhearted generosity.

It was not surprising that the Prince had an inconsistent nature, for he suffered under a father who hated and loved him, simultaneously. Therefore, the Prince surrounded himself with cronies who agreed with him and dismissed any friendship of long standing at the slightest displeasure. His whims were legion and excessive, his sentimentality, verbose and maudlin.

This impulsive and open nature encouraged an overwhelming atmosphere of romance. Once smitten, his heart knew no bounds of adoration, and he would declare himself the slave to Cupid's dictates. The liaison and rumored marriage to Mrs.

Fitzherbert were well-known, but his latest para-
mour was Lady Jersey, an attractive grandmother.
He seemed to seek and need pampering comforts
from his mistresses. He generally avoided dalli-
ances with younger women, and although he might
flirt with them for vanity's sake, his real interest
lay in a mothering relationship.

While his faults were numerous, he could be credited to be the first Hanover with excellent taste, an
eye for beauty and good design. His interests were
furniture, works of art, silver, and architecture. He
indulged in wine and food, and he adored clothes.

Embarking on a lifetime of renovating and build-
ing, he transformed Carlton House into a glorious
showplace, to the hue and cry of the public due to
his outrageous debts.

The circle of friends known as the Carlton Set
were generally a rather ramshackle contingent,
indulging in much drinking, gambling, and other
crude diversions. Therefore, many of the more
conservative members of the *ton* discreetly avoided
his entertainments.

On occasion, however, the Prince held proper
gatherings in an effort to align some members of
the aristocracy to his side, while his father moved
in and out of periods of madness. These aristocrats
were well aware that one day he would be king, and
one must not offend.

On this fine, spring evening, the Prince,
resplendent in dress and dazzling medals, stood
greeting his guests on just such a sedate occasion.
The ballroom was teeming with beautifully gowned
ladies and their equally sartorial husbands. The
magnificent room was ablaze with glittering
candles and sparkling jewels.

Arriving with Lord Stewart, Mary Beth and Angel
were almost lost in the crush of guests. The tip of

Angel's head was barely visible among the forest of shoulders as Lord Stewart guided them into the crowd.

They were observed entering by the Marquess of Kendall, who stood talking with several lords of the realm. He watched as Lord Stewart and his family were received by the enthusiastic Prince.

Too enthusiastic, Ward observed. Apprehension crept through his body. Damn, Stewart's a fool, he thought. Lady Angel was fast becoming the reigning toast of the Season and the old, reprobate Prince would not resist using his imagined charms on her. He was never above attempting seduction on any young or middle-aged lady. Leighton's eyes narrowed and his body stiffened. If Stewart was so obtuse, there was no choice but to keep an eye on things himself.

Although his reputation had kept him safe from the bonds of matrimony, Lord Leighton suddenly regretted it. He was accepted everywhere young ladies were chaperoned, the result of which did not allow him to whisk Lady Harlan away without tarnishing her name. Why in the devil was he concerning himself? he wondered. Still, he was drawn, so he continued to keep careful watch in the obscurity of conversation among the group of men.

The Prince greeted Lord Stewart, "Ah, Farnham, I see you bring me spring flowers to grace Carlton House." He gave a cursory nod to Mary Beth, then turned his eager eyes to Angel.

There is no doubt who is the flower and who is the weed, Mary Beth thought, more than a little bemused.

The Prince of Wales' scrutiny was more of an ogle as he regarded Angel's porcelain skin, brilliant eyes, and sweet smile. She looked alluring with her flaxen curls tumbling about her slender neck, one errant ringlet falling over her shoulder and resting on an expanse of ivory skin.

Lady Harlan instantly reminded him of his *Venus*, a recently acquired miniature copy of Jacopo Sansovino. He squeezed Lady Harlan's hand with his moist plump one at that provocative thought.

Angel may have reminded the Prince of Venus, but Mary Beth thought he resembled a bug-eyed toad about to pounce on a June bug. Mary Beth snapped her fan open and began to fan in agitation. She glanced at her father and thought he looked like a lackey buffoon by Bruegel with his smile of sub-jugated affability.

"Your name suits you well," Prinny purred as he raised Angel from her deep curtsy, sure that his lofty pronouncement was the highlight of the girl's Season.

"You are too kind. I consider it high praise and, as the proud grandparent, must concur," Lord Stewart interjected.

The Prince chuckled. "Perhaps we'll speak later," he said in a caressing voice as he turned to greet his next guest.

"Angel, you be wary of the Prince. He imagines he is irresistible to all ladies," Mary Beth whispered.

"You're not serious?" Angel laughed in nervous disbelief. "He's positively ancient."

"I am very serious." Mary Beth replied.

The evening did not improve as the rooms became positively oppressive. Allowing no open windows against the night air, demanding fires in every hearth lest he catch a chill, the Prince assured his guests unbearable discomfort.

Angel and Mary Beth trailed Lord Stewart in growing dismay. No amount of fanning could relieve the heat. While being introduced to various guests, Angel tried to keep a smile on her face as the perspiration trickled down her back.

Angel almost jumped when she heard the Prince's voice, for she had not seen his approach.

"Do me the honor of walking with me a bit. I should like to visit with you and find out how you are enjoying the Season," Prinny commanded.

Angel curtsied and, reluctantly, took his proffered arm. She glanced at Mary Beth, who stood with closed, tight lips and a darkening expression in her eyes. Lord Stewart beamed with pride at the royal notice Angel had achieved, and nodded approval.

Lord Leighton continued his survey of the proceedings, unnoticed by Angel or her family. The fool Prince would think Angel positively drooling over his consequence, Ward thought, and feared the worst. He frowned. The stupidity surpassed understanding. He had never taken Stewart for a flat, but he was obviously unaware of the Prince's intentions. Stewart looked the fool in his eagerness to have his granddaughter accepted. Why couldn't Stewart see she was doing very well without the Prince's "help?" Ward was annoyed, for here he was playing the champion again. If she left the room on the Prince's arm, there would be a vulgar titillation among those assembled.

Realizing he could not openly protect her or she would be immediately cast as his latest mistress, he shook his head. Damn, he thought, Needs must when the devil drives, and so he would conceal his actions and see that she came to no harm. Damn, Ward cursed again, he would be the villain in this piece before the tale ended. He excused himself just as Angel disappeared from sight on the Prince's arm.

Ward crossed the room and nodded to Mary Beth as he passed. He could not be sure she understood, but he hoped she did. When he entered the hall, it was empty, except for footmen who stood at various posts. He paused, wondering where in the hell Prinny had taken Lady Angel. Every nerve in his body was tense and each sense alert. He strode along the hall hoping to hear some conversation at best, a scream at worse. If he were to play the hero, it ought to at least be done in style, he mused.

He paused in indecision. The art gallery! Prinny is boastful of his collection. Ward increased the speed of his steps. Familiar with Carlton House, his way was sure. He blushed with chagrin when he thought of some of the raucous nights he had spent here. Alas, not even he could undo those regrettable evenings, and now that way of life might keep him from . . . He did not allow himself the completion of the thought.

He entered a magnificent gallery, housing some of the finest paintings in all Europe. For all his buffoonery, the Prince had an eye for beauty. The thought was no comfort to Ward with the image of Angel in his mind.

Angel marveled at the number of magnificent paintings. Prinny guided her through the gallery into an anteroom off the side of the great hall. The fact that she went without demur was amazing. In truth, Angel simply did not know how to refuse the Prince. He was awesome and Angel unsure.

The Prince was perspiring heavily from the brisk walk through the halls. Angel wondered at the creaking noise emanating from his royal personage between the sounds of wheezing breaths. She knew nothing of cumberland corsets, but decided then and there that she could outrun him.

"My dear, you must see this exquisite bronze," the Prince panted. Angel felt a considerable sympathy for the elderly gentleman. Her grandfather was more fit than the Prince of Wales!

Prinny lumbered over to an inlaid cabinet and extracted a truly magnificent work of art. Angel had never in all her life seen a naked body. She hardly saw her own, and that only during the brief moments while bathing. She had never looked at herself in a mirror. One was taught not to think about bodies, let alone speak of them or view them. Mesdames Whiterspoons would have fainted on the spot at such a thought. Her nannies had been of the same mind.

Angel was made of sterner fabric. She did not faint; instead, she turned beet red. What does one say? Her mind scrambled quickly to find something appropriate. Mary Beth's warning crystalized in her mind. This time, there was no laughter.

"I wanted you to see this particularly. I should imagine the artist had someone very much like you in mind. In fact, upon meeting you, I thought of this treasure," the Prince said, eyeing her body with a licentious smile.

Angel backed away as he handed it to her. She refused to take it.

"Have I offended you? I should think not. I'm sure you recognize great art," he said, rather shocked by her missish behavior. Her mother had been quite open-minded.

Angel had managed to move so that a table separated them. The Prince moved to the right. Angel moved to the left. The effort was reversed.

The Prince stopped and gasped for his breath, studying her a moment. He saw a glowering scowl replace the benign expression and two small hands curled into fists.

At that moment the gods smiled upon Angel, for a voice broke the embarrassed moment. "Your Royal highness, Lord Leighton is asking for you. He is quite distraught. Something he claims is of the most critical nature. He awaits you as soon as you can possibly return," a footman exclaimed, entering the room with a new gold crown in his pocket, which apparently overcame the trepidation of his interruption.

"Excuse me, my dear, I shall return immediately. Wait, there is something I wish to ask you. I think you have misunderstood me, and I should repine at such a thought. So wait upon my return," the Prince said as he smiled and bowed with the attending creak.

The minute he moved through the door, Angel scampered to the French doors of the balcony. She slid behind the draperies, opened the door slightly, and squeezed through the narrow opening.

She found herself on an ornamental balcony of wrought iron, which had never been built for functional use. There was barely room for her, and if she had weighed a stone more, it might have given way.

With a hammering heart, Angel knew she had to make good a fast escape. The sobering thought of backtracking into the arms of the lecherous Prince sent waves of revulsion through her body. She studied the overhanging branches of the elm. Could she do it? She had climbed many a tree in her youth, but never in a ball gown.

She heard sounds in the room. Thinking it to be the Prince, she panicked. She took a deep breath and reached out for the branch. Hanging on for dear life, Angel swung her leg over to the limb and issued a prayer for divine deliverance. It would take as much to extricate her from this predicament.

Straddling the branch, she caught her breath. Now to get down and then find Mary Beth. Her grandfather would have her head. She looked around and noticed the grounds were not empty. There were casual strollers or lovers scattered about.

"Great Scott, I could be here all hours. No one must find me. Now I've done it! Grandfather will kill me. I promised never to make a scene." Tears stung her eyes when she realized the gravity of her situation. Don't panic, she told herself. Think of something!

She edged her way down the branch toward the trunk and into more cover of the leaves. She heard the terrifying sound of ripping fabric. Closing her eyes, she hung on for dear life. The life of a spinster, she surmised. The thought made her smile, if only briefly. Anything would be better than running from fat, lecherous old men. I'll join a nunnery!

Leighton glanced around the empty rooms for Lady Angel. Where had she gone? He dare not ask the Prince where he had misplaced Lord Stewart's granddaughter. He wanted no scene, for undoubtedly Lady Angel would fade from Prinny's mind as soon as he rejoined his guests. He did not want the Prince to sound the alarm for missing Lady Angel Harlan. Lord, that's all she would need to end her Season, and for some unknown reason, he did not want that to happen to her.

Taking what he was sure was enough time so as not to cause attention, he retraced his footsteps and again entered the antechamber off the gallery. He stood at the door. This time he scanned the room more carefully and noticed the velvet draperies had obviously been disturbed. Closing the door and

crossing the room, he drew back the drape *Burton* and
peered out.

There she was, perched on a branch—somewhat
hidden to be sure—but by God, she had climbed the
tree to get away from Prinny! A smile of admiration
crossed his face.

He dared not put his weight on the decorative
balcony.

"Hold tight, I'll be there," he called in a stage
whisper.

Angel peered up. She couldn't be sure it was Lord
Leighton, so she did not reply.

"Wait quietly," he said, and turned to make his
way out of the room. He sauntered down the hall,
stopping briefly to speak to various acquaintances.
His feet wished to fly, but he calmly made his way
so as not to attract attention. He did not want
anyone to remember precisely where he had been
or gone. Retrieving his evening cape, he eventually
made his way down the steps and out into the small
garden below the French windows.

There were a few strollers but none near at this
moment.

He moved silently to stand beneath the tree. "My
lady, it's Leighton here. See if you can move down
and I'll catch you."

"I can barely see," she whispered.

"Move carefully and don't speak. I don't want
anyone to find us."

She nodded silently and felt for the next branch.
Ward could hear rustling and a few grunts.

The pale moonlight softly reflected on her dress.

"I'm just below you. Jump," he ordered.

Jump into the black of night that spread before
her like the inside of a crypt! Her pulse drummed
in her ears as her sweaty palms moved along the
rough bark. Edging forward, she could just see

Ward's outline against the faint light from the windows.

"I see you now," she whispered.

"Quiet! Jump," he again ordered.

She did. The sound of rent fabric pierced the air. Ward grabbed her waist as she slid down and held on for dear life while they both tumbled to the ground. She let out a squeal and he a grunt as the wind was knocked out of him.

"You have the impact of an elephant," he muttered.

They lay stunned for a moment. Ward had her grasped tightly, feeling her soft feminine body with growing pleasure.

Angel raised her head in suspicion and whispered, "Did you intend to rescue me to this position?"

"The idea is infinitely appealing. I suspect the results would be more permanent than you might wish." He softly laughed.

Taking her hand, he raised them both and led her down a slight incline among overhanging lilacs, just as a pair of lovers came strolling down the walk. Ward and Angel could hear their voices floating clearly on the night air.

"Did you hear something funny?"

"Yes. What do you think it is?" the female asked, as she clutched her brave gallant for protection.

The lovers seated themselves on a charming wrought-iron bench made in a swan motif. Prinny and his artifice, Ward thought.

"Sit just a moment, please. There's something I must ask," the male pleaded in a voice of undeniable urgency.

"Well, I'm not sure. If you think it's proper . . . My father . . ." the lady sighed.

Ward grimaced. Good Lord, now, what?

As she cowered under the branches of the heavenly scented lilacs, Angel's legs began cramping, so she sat upon the dewy ground. The moisture reached her skin. What next? she thought in dismay.

Angel knew her dress was torn beyond repair, her hair tumbled down over her shoulders. All semblance of a coiffure was gone.

Ward pulled her close, his cape covering them. The black fabric offered considerable protection from being detected.

Ward could feel the slender body of Lady Harlan. She felt tantalizing. They could not move, talk, or leave until Romeo posed his question and left. The intensity of her nearness increased.

Angel, pinned close to Lord Leighton, became equally aware of the muscled body pressed next to her. She could feel his breath on her cheek and his strong arm around her. She flushed. A hot, tingling, sensation spread through her body.

Ward Leighton was no less affected by the soft, shapely body pressed against him, and his heart began to pound. He couldn't move, lest he give them away, and he didn't want to. Here he was with a lady in so compromising a position that, if found, he would have to marry her. And he did not want to move!

The couple's voices continued.

"Pamela, you must accept my suit. I adore you. 'Come live with me and be my love, and we will all the pleasures prove. That valleys, groves, hills, and fields, woods or steepy mountains yield.' "

"Oh, Reginald, you wrote that for me? You are so wonderful and talented," she sighed happily.

Reginald had the decency to blush, but he did not want to spoil any illusions.

"If only my father would consent, Reginald," whined Pamela.

"If I just knew what to do," Reginald said.

"Suppose I boldly put my suit to your father. My inheritance will come to me in the autumn," Reginald said.

"Oh, Reginald, you are so clever. Yes, that's the very thing. You are so clever," Pamela answered as if the idea had been his.

"Great heavens, go ask him and get the hell out of here," Ward whispered under his breath. He had no intentions of Angel hearing him. He had muttered it to himself.

Angel could feel his lips so close to her cheek while they dare not move, and she heard his oath.

Ward felt her body begin to shake. His arm tightened. She is going to giggle, he thought.

Angel, suddenly overcome with this insane situation, could not suppress the growing mirth. Ward placed his mouth over hers in a desperate effort to silence her.

Scientific annals do not mention this miraculous cure, but Angel's giggles subsided instantly. A weak protest faded into a gentle response. Ward continued to kiss her, not stopping with the cessation of her laughter.

"Darling, let us go at once and ask your father, together," Reginald announced, relieved with the comforting prospect of feminine protection against a possible tyrant. Standing up, he took the hand of his beloved and led her toward the ballroom.

Ward and Angel remained quiet a few moments longer. Ward rose, grateful for the black night.

Angel, blushing with fiery emotion, was equally thankful for the darkness.

Ward wrapped his cape about her and drew her near. He bent to whisper, "You understand, I had to keep you from laughing. I meant no offense or liberty."

"I understand; there was nothing but my safety involved in the kiss. Do not consider it again," she primly replied.

For some reason Ward blanched, the answer did not please him.

"Wait in the shadows. Do not move. I'll get the carriage and see you home safely."

6

Leighton vainly attempted to brush the grass and leaves from his once-impeccable evening attire. Checking to see that Lady Harlan was remaining just where he had left her, he proceeded down the walk, skirting the light cast from the windows. He hurried, wondering every step of the way just how he was going to accomplish getting her home. Surely she was beginning to be missed inside.

He paused in the shadows, and by some miraculous stroke of coincidental, phenomenal luck, Major-General MacDougal was crossing the gravel drive toward the waiting carriages.

"Psst, psst, Duncan," Ward whispered from the shadows. MacDougal halted his stride and looked about. "Here by the walk. It's Leighton. Come here."

MacDougal, who had led forages at Assayc and Argaum against the Mahrattas under Wellesley with cool dispatch, was dumbfounded. He walked slowly to the dim figure furtively lingering in the shadows.

Even in the faint light, he could see a very disheveled Lord Leighton.

"Dash it, man, you play the rapscallion fobbing

a pinched gold watch from an alley," MacDougal said.

Ward chuckled. "You can't imagine the unlikely situation in which I find myself."

"Involving the fairer sex, I presume," MacDougal chided with a soft laugh.

"I've played the gallant and saved an incredibly innocent from the clutches of Prinny."

"Among the shrubbery?" Duncan asked.

"So it seems. Now, here is what I need you to do without any undue notice. It is imperative that all seems quite normal, or a vulnerable young lady will be falsely ostracized. And well you know, my name must not be connected with this episode," Ward said.

"That shouldn't be too hard to accomplish. You have hardly made your reputation in the saving of ladies' virtue," MacDougal good-naturedly chided.

"Exactly my predicament," Ward sighed. "Go fetch Lady Mary Beth Stewart and tell her Lady Harlan was taken ill and returned home. There's the problem. Why wouldn't she seek her aunt herself, and with whom did she return? Do you think we could conjure up a bishop to have done the honorable duty?" Ward asked in desperation and certainly not seriously.

Major-General MacDougal let out a small gasp of air, "Lady Stewart. Yes, I am acquainted with her. For the life of me I can't think of a plausible answer."

Ward shrugged. "Simply say she returned but you don't know the details. I'll think of something, I hope."

Sitting with his head against the velvet squabs, Leighton closed his eyes to gather his thoughts.

Angel, clutching his lordship's cape to cover her
demolished dress, sat in quiet dismay. The rhythm
of the horses hooves were comforting, for they led
her home to relative safety, if she were ever able
to extricate herself from her grandfather's pre-
dictable wrath.

"You have an uncanny aptitude for disaster, Lady
Harlan. No wonder your grandfather wants you
safely wed. Your gentle demeanor hopefully will
take in some poor unsuspecting soul who can suffer
the efforts to contain you."

Angel did not reply. She glanced at his shadowy
profile.

Suddenly he turned. "Did the Prince actually
offend you? I mean, did he accost you?"

"Well, not precisely. He pursued me around a
table, insisting I look at some silly statue of Venus,
which he disgustingly compared me to."

"Ah, I know the one. I apologize for the Prince's
stupidity. Did it shock your sensibilities? Are you
still appalled?" he asked kindly and with concern.

"You mean because she has no clothing?"

"Precisely."

"Actually, I suppose I was embarrassed, but can
you imagine comparing me to that?"

"It is beautiful. You were insulted?"

"Of course. Did you ever see the size of her hips?"

Leighton was so taken aback he was speechless.

"The size of her hips?"

"They are more than ample, far more."

It was Leighton's turn to laugh, "Angel . . . pardon
me, Lady Harlan, you never cease to amaze me."

"Well, it was unjust and most uncomplimentary.
When the Prince said he would return to ask me
something, after your request to see him, I took the
only way to escape I could find."

"You mean you could not have simply walked out the door, through the gallery, and back to the reception hall?"

The censure was pointed and demeaning. Angel thought, He hadn't been chased around a table. However, she recognized that she might have been a bit hasty to go out a window, and she tried desperately to justify her stupidity.

"I didn't think of that. I only wanted to escape."

"Well, you accomplished that feat. Now, what do we do?" he asked.

"You mean my grandfather."

"Yes, you can hardly let it be known I've escorted you home in total dishabille. My reputation does not allow that privilege, unfortunately." His voice was gentle.

"No, I suppose not. They're probably frantic by now."

"I've sent a friend of mine, Major-General MacDougal, to inform your aunt and grandfather of your sudden illness. He is to say you returned home," Ward said with a smooth voice that masked his concern. She had experienced enough for one evening and he didn't want her to suffer any more than was necessary. He just wanted her safely out of this situation with no harm done.

"With whom?" she asked.

"With whom what?" he asked, not understanding.

"Did I return?" she asks.

"That is the first problem now facing us," he sighed.

"What's the second?"

"How to get you into the house unseen."

They sat in silence for several moments.

"Lord Leighton, why don't we just pretend I fell off the balcony? I could have just lain there. It would explain my torn dress and hair, I suppose?"

"Angel, er, Lady Harlan, we can not choose that route. If you look at yourself, you'd know a mere fall from the top of Saint Paul's, let alone the balcony at Carlton House, could not result in such dishevel. You look as though you've been mauled by an invading army," he replied with a laugh.

Angel was at a loss for a solution.

"If the family scandal did not follow me about, I should be able to act more openly," Angel said.

"Perhaps that's so, but I believe you are under no more restrictions than most young ladies your age," he replied with logic.

"You can do as you please," she said.

"There you are completely mistaken. But we will not discuss my position, it is with yours that we concern ourselves. Tell me who will be up, where they would most likely be, and are any back entrances left open?"

"Jefferies will be nodding off on a chair in the foyer. The rest of the servants will have gone to bed. There is the mews road behind the garden. The door to the wall might be open or it might be locked, I'm not sure."

"What of your abigail?"

"I can trust Jeanne. She'll burn my dress. Of course, I'm going to be in a devil of a corner trying to find a way to explain its disappearance. I suppose I could trust Mary Beth also," Angel said softly. These events were beginning to weigh a bit heavily.

Lord Leighton leaned out of the carriage window and directed his coachman to the mews road behind the Stewart town house.

"I thought I would choke when that stupid lady thought he was reciting his own poetry. I suppose she's never read Shakespeare," Angel said with a giggle.

"Marlowe," Leighton replied.

"Marlowe! Are you sure?" Angel asked, annoyed.

"I'll take a wager on it," he replied.

"You're as smug as that foolish young man being manipulated by the young lady."

"Smug?"

"Certainly, he believed everything she said about his being clever and wonderful. That's the caliber of young men available from which to choose a husband. A sorry lot to be sure. I think I'll remain single," Angel said.

"You mean my night's work has gone for naught? Had I left you hanging in the tree, you probably would have been claimed daft and not given a chance to wed," he said in a peal of laughter.

"I am grateful for your rescue. I would prefer not to seem daft," she said with a merry laugh of her own.

When the laughter subsided, silence united them as each pondered the problem at hand.

Arriving at their destination, Ward turned to Angel and said, "May luck be with us. We don't have much time. Your family is surely by now en route."

He assisted her down from the coach and took her arm as he reached for the wall gate. It opened with a slight, complaining creak, causing Ward to chuckle. "Hopefully an omen to our luck."

Angel clutched his cloak about her and scampered alongside her champion. When they reached the back entrance, he put his arm around her and paused.

"We might try the French doors on the terrace," she whispered.

Hovering close in the shadows, they slid along the edge of the terrace to the doors. Angel tried the handle. The door was locked. She turned to him helplessly just as the moon appeared from behind a cloud. The silver beams lit her pale hair like a shining halo. Her eyes were wide with fear.

Ward's heart leapt at the poignant, innocent face. He desired nothing more than to draw her to him. It was a sweet torment, an anguish of desire and need, and he had never experienced such a dramatic reaction before.

"Do you want me to stay? I can vouch for what happened. I do think, or at least hope, your grandfather would believe our story. It's just that my amorous adventures are highly overrated, and I don't think you need my reputation casting incorrect speculation. I will stay to defend you if you think it best." Lord Leighton spoke with an inner regret that was not apparent.

"No, you should not be involved. These things get out. The servants will know the whole of it by morning. Since they gossip as much as their masters, it will be general knowledge among the *ton* by afternoon."

"You are sure?" he asked.

"Great heavens, we wouldn't want you to be the poor unsuspecting soul that has to wed me, now, would we?" she dryly said.

Ward did not reply. He pressed his shoulder against the door and gave a hefty heave to the sound of splintering wood.

"Tell Lord Stewart to install more substantial locks, since you were able to merely press against the door for it to give way," he said, believing all this was sounding more incredible by the moment.

"I'll tell him I gave a shove with my hips," she teased.

Lord Leighton laughed. He drew her to him and kissed her cheek. "Good luck, minx. I stand in your service. Call me if you have need of my help, but

please stay out of impossible tangles. I'm too old
to rescue innocents."

Angel handed him his cape and looked up into his
face. The planes of his face were barely visible and
she could not see the expression in his eyes. She
wanted to reach out and hug him, but dared not.

"Thank you, my lord," she simply said, and slid
into the house. She stood in the dark room and
watched him disappear into the night. She was
bereft with the idea that he must think her a fool.

Silently making her way to her room through the
back hall and stairs, she wept with humiliation,
regret, and some unkown feeling of loss. When she
entered her room, Jeanne rose with a gasp.

"Lady Angel! What has happened? Are you
injured?" she wailed, her hands pressed against her
face.

"Oh, hurry, help me out of this dress," Angel tear-
fully pleaded as she struggled to remove the combs
from her hair.

Jeanne complied in stunned silence.

Angel rolled up the dress and threw it under her
bed. She ran to the dressing table and picked up her
silver brush. "Fetch me water," she ordered as she
furiously ran the brush through her tangled hair.
She cringed when she removed some leaves stuck
in the tangled mass of curls.

Jeanne stood watching in fascinated silence.

Angel frowned. "Don't stand there! Help me wash
my face and hands."

They were accomplishing this very feat when
Angel heard the carriage in the drive. Her hands
flew. She managed to remove the dirt from her face
and hands. All leaves were accounted for. Her mind
was in ferment as she brushed furiously.

Jeanne gasped, "Your slippers!"

Angel glanced down, they were covered with mud,

as was the hem of her petticoat. Jeanne knelt, untied the shoes, and rolled her eyes when she saw the ruined stockings. There was no end to the damage done to Angel's clothing.

"Jeanne, I ran away from the Prince. He was rude," Angel finally said when stripping off the muddy, ripped stockings.

Just as Angel united her petticoat, the door burst open and Mary Beth entered. She stopped dead in her tracks. Her eyes narrowed.

"Jeanne, leave us," Mary Beth ordered.

Jeanne bobbed a curtsy and scampered out. Lordy, lordy, the abigail thought, there was going to be trouble this night and she did not wish to be at hand.

"You are ill?" Mary Beth hissed.

"No. Aunt Mary Beth, just let me explain."

"You look a sight! And I presume you've been making hasty improvements to your appearance. Your grandfather is furious and wants to see you immediately in his study."

"Oh, Mary Beth, it was awful," Angel wailed. "The Prince chased me and I ran away." She managed a stream of tears as she rung her hands.

"Save your theatrics for your grandfather, Angel, and whatever tale you have to tell. You foolish child! Luckily, no one knows anything about the mysterious disappearance of Lady Harlan. The gods smile on you. Let's see if Grandfather does."

Angel removed her petticoat. She looked horrified when she noticed her muddy feet. Her eyes met those of Mary Beth's and she wanted to die.

"Quickly, make yourself presentable!"

"Didn't the major-general tell you I was ill?" Shouldn't I be in bed?" Angel asked hopefully.

"Yes, but I didn't believe it. I knew you were in some scrape or other."

"What does Grandfather believe?" Angel asked.

"He's not sure, but he's ready to come down heavy. Kept saying in the carriage, over and over, 'She should have called for us. There's a pack of humbug here.' "

"He did?" Angel asked with a worried frown as she donned a pristine nightdress. She picked up her soiled petticoat and stockings and threw them under the bed.

"I assume the dress is there also."

Angel nodded forlornly. "Do I look passable now?" she asked.

"Angel Harlan, your mother named you well. You look as innocent as a saint. Your story had better be as good, or he'll have your head on a platter."

Lord Stewart's face was the color of a turnip, white in the middle and purple on the edges. His obvious rage made Angel's knees buckle for a moment.

He watched her entrance. She was as white as a sheet and she seemed unsteady. Perhaps there was an explanation, he reasoned.

"Well, girl, out with it! Why did you leave without informing us? What happened? Are you ill? Who brought you home?"

Angel's head whirled and out came a tale of half-truths and whole lies.

She explained that the Prince had chased her around a table trying to kiss her, and he had showed her a naked statue. That would enrage her grandfather and bring sympathy to her. She had made an escape from a balcony and had ripped her dress; therefore, she could not return to the ballroom. She ran through the muddy garden and hailed a hackney carriage to take her home. Afraid of the servants seeing her, she had pushed her way into the library through the French doors and scurried up the back stairs so no one would see her. Angel sighed and looked up at her grandfather through veiled lashes to see if he believed her.

"How did Major-General MacDougal come to know you were ill?" Lord Stewart asked.

Angel gulped. "MacDougal? Oh, that must be the soldier I called. I told him to fetch you home," she lied.

Mary Beth looked pale as she watched the proceedings. How much was true? And Major-General MacDougal? She sighed a weary sigh.

Lord Stewart sat a moment. He studied the innocent face of his granddaughter and was chagrined at his part in allowing her to go off with the old reprobate Prince. His own guilt allowed him not to examine the tale more clearly.

"You were incredibly foolish. We all were," he sighed. "But no harm was done. I do not think anyone knows you were missing."

Angel stood horrified. They were as convinced as she was appalled at her lies.

Later, having been excused, she lay ensconced in her bed. She stared at the ceiling and relived each incredulous moment. Twice she had acted without thought of consequence. She had a habit of doing that, and she had to stop. It only proved her stupid and it courted disaster. Lord Leighton must think her an utter ninny, despite his kindness. She could never redeem herself in his eyes. She knew she was condemned to disdain from the worldly, handsome, gallant gentleman. If she could just tell him she wasn't a ninny . . . But telling wouldn't make him believe. She would have to prove she was very sensible and proper.

To what purpose? she wondered. She wanted his

esteem. She closed her eyes and felt his lips on hers again. She flushed with pleasure at the remembered strength of his arms. Tears rolled down her cheeks; she would always be condemned the fool in his eyes.

7

The night, Angel reasoned, was as close to purgatory as a person could get. Dreams of running helplessly through a garden mixed with those of a panting prince, a pair of blue-green eyes, and a confusing struggle to escape. There were dreams of safety in Lord Leighton's arms, which faded almost as soon as they appeared, leaving a feeling of chagrin.

She awoke tangled among the covers, her heart pounding and her body damp with perspiration. Several moments passed before the panic subsided. Desperately trying to bring some semblance to her scattered wits, she methodically reviewed the previous evening's events. Recalling each moment, her emotions ranged from a recognition of her stupidity to the still-existing problems created by her half-truths and lies.

Major-General MacDougal must be informed of the "role" he played. She could imagine her grandfather effusively thanking the general for his assistance when his granddaughter was taken ill! She shuddered with vision of the general's ensuing pregnant pause and blank stare.

"Lies begat lies," she exclaimed. Struggling from the covers, she bounced out of bed. Lord Leighton must be informed on just what she had told her grandfather.

Dashing across the room, she threw open the draperies to the first, pink light of dawn. The servants would soon be stirring. So little sleep! If that is what one could call her tortured dreams. Could she accomplish all that must be done? There was no time to lose.

She scurried to Jeanne's adjoining room and roughly aroused the sleeping abigail. No consideration was given to Jeanne's peaceful sleep, for time and secrecy were of the utmost importance.

"Jeanne, you must do something for me. Dress quickly," Angel commanded.

The young maid struggled to consciousness in a pitiful fog of disorientation.

"Whatever is wrong at this hour?" she said, coming to appreciate the panic in her mistress's voice.

"You must carry a letter for me to Lord Leighton. It is imperative! Oh, Jeanne, you must help me," Angel wailed.

Jeanne stared in dismay. Lady Harlan was the best of mistresses and never had she begged for a service. Her eyes widened and apprehension loomed. After last evening's obvious scrape, more trouble would be courted by carrying a letter to Lord Leighton.

"You mean for me to carry a letter to Lord Leighton?" she asked, her lips trembling. The image of Lord Stewart dismissing her on the spot took shape.

"Yes, I shall write the note while you quickly dress. You must go at once, before the servants begin the day," Angel said, already halfway out of the doorway and heading directly to her desk.

With a pounding heart, Jeanne scampered along the sidewalk in the light morning fog. The first rays of sunlight streamed through the misty air, giving an eerie sensation to this covert mission. Clutching her cloak, she hurried her steps. A few servants were about, but for the most part the streets were empty.

Pale with fright, she continued on with her mistress's scandalous orders. Trembling with fear of discovery and torn by her fierce loyalty, she knew this outlandish task was crucial, or Lady Harlan would not have insisted.

By the time she reached her destination, the sun glowed on the rooftops and the remnants of fog trailed along the curbs like whisps of smoke. Breathlessly reaching the gate leading to Lord Leighton's door, she glanced along the street in both directions. There were no witnesses to her arrival. Pulling her hood closer to her face, she timidly raised the door knocker. It seemed forever, but finally the door opened.

"Is Lord Leighton in?" Jeanne asked in the barest whisper.

"Certainly not to visitors," the arrogant footman answered, rubbing his sleepy eyes. His watch shift was ending, but he had spent the last few hours snoring in a foyer chair.

"I have a very important letter to give your master," she said.

"I will see he gets it," he said, and extended his hand.

"I'm to give it to Lord Leighton," she stammered.

"Ain't possible," the footman replied. He was both annoyed and interested.

Jeanne shifted. What should she do? She frowned at Angel's suggestion that she faint, if necessary, to gain admittance.

"I must see him," she said with rising vexation.

"If ye want me to give him the letter, I will. If not, be off with ye," he said, stepping back to shut the door.

"Who is it?" The voice was low and resonant.

The startled footman turned to see Lord Leighton crossing the hall.

"A maid with some message," he said, stepping back.

Jeanne blinked her eyes. There stood Lord Leighton in riding attire, looking like a Greek god. She blushed as she removed the crisp, sealed letter from her cape. She handed it to his lordship, curtsied, and ran down the steps as if the hounds of hell were after her.

Watching the taciturn reception of the letter and the casual saunter of his lordship, the footman shrugged his shoulders. It was probably just a message from another ladylove.

Closing the study door, Ward warily opened the missive. His eyes scanned the hastily written, ink-spotted letter. Interest turned to dismay, then to amusement as a smile lit his eyes and crinkled their corners. The contents revealed a rambling account of the story Lady Harlan had told her grandfather. At no time, she reassured him, did she mention his name. She went on to mention that some unknown gentleman, Major-General MacDougal, had carried the message to her grandfather when she had been taken "ill." He had also helped in obtaining a hackney carriage for the return home. She then requested that he inform Major-General MacDougal

on the facts of his "assistance," or all would be lost.
Could he arrange for the gentleman to call in
feigned solicitude? She stated that by his doing so,
she was sure her grandfather would believe her.

Ward shook his head. She was correct, of course.
Under those circumstances any gentleman would
pay a call of concern. The lady was a devilish
handful, and he wondered how she had managed
to survive childhood. It was obvious that she had
an uncanny sense for extricating herself from mis-
adventure. One would have to have the eyes and
hands of a Buddha to play her yeoman of the guard.
Tossing the letter into the fireplace, he decided to
postpone his ride and call on Duncan regardless of
the hour.

Angel hurried through her own toilette. She had
been dressed by a maid all her life, and the task
proved frustrating. As she struggled with a million
tiny buttons and stubborn, wayward curls, a bead
of perspiration broke out from her upper lip and
forehead. She swore a soft oath at her fumbling
efforts. In hopes of achieving a serene look of the
innocent to dispel last evening's episode from everyone's mind, she struggled on, calculating her appearance could not be accomplished without
Jeanne. There could be no suspicion as to her
maid's whereabouts.

She appraised the results with satisfaction. Her
dress was white lawn with a high-waisted bodice.
The frilled neck and wrap-over front enhanced her
angelic look. The skirt was designed with an apron
front and tied around the waist in a bow. The top
sleeves were short and narrow, the lower sleeves
extended over her hands. Angel studied the narrow
lines of the skirt with pleasure, for the dress tended
to give her some height. Movement was easier with

the disappearance of the train for daytime, and considering her anxiety, she was grateful, for surely she would trip over one.

Taking up her shawl, she wrapped it tightly to her body. The chill she felt was fear, and it was numbing. The intermittent warm flushes that spread across her cheeks were from the thought of the mounting lies over a totally unnecessary situation.

The wait seemed endless as she paced back and forth. The serenity she sought eluded her and the blue shadows beneath her eyes gave away her fretful night. The clock ticked on and on. She looked at it again and again.

Finally, Jeanne slipped into her room. So relieved, Angel hugged her tightly, not knowing whether to laugh or cry.

"Did anyone see you leave or return?" Angel asked.

"I don't think so," Jeanne replied, almost in tears.

"Did he get the letter?"

"Yes, I put it into his very hands."

"Thank you, thank you. You have saved my life. Now, do not breathe a word. Swear to it, by all that is holy," Angel commanded.

"I'll not tell a soul, but I'm happy I'll not have to do that again," Jeanne said, still trembling.

"Never, I swear," Angel promised as she ran to her wardrobe. Pulling out a particularly charming sprigged muslin gown, she thrust it into Jeanne's arms.

"Here, take it. It will become you for Sunday church and all." Angel wasn't even sure what servants did on Sunday or their time off. Maybe Jeanne could use the dress. The thought struck Angel that her life had been too narrow. She would think about that when this coil was straightened out.

Jeanne fingered the soft fabric with pleasure.

Major-General MacDougal was enjoying a hearty breakfast when Lord Leighton called. The many years of disciplined army life were etched into MacDougal's daily habits. While the rest of genteel society slept, MacDougal was well into his day.

"Come in and join me for a bit of breakfast," Duncan said as his valet ushered Ward into the dining room.

"Don't mind if I do. I suddenly realize I'm hungry."

"Well, what brings you at this hour of morning? It was my understanding you gadabouts slept the morning away," Duncan teased.

Leighton laughed. "Never was one to sleep in the morning, although I suppose I've been considered a gadabout."

"Every member of the *ton* should spend a year in the army. Toughen them up a bit, I should think. The Prince of Wales is a prime example. Never saw a man go to fat as quickly as he," Duncan said as a plate of ham, eggs, kippers, and sweet rolls was placed before Leighton by an unobtrusive servant.

"It's done by eating mountains of wonderful-looking food such as this," Ward said in mock consternation.

"You exercise, for there's not an ounce of fat on you," Duncan said approvingly.

"Prinny gives me inspiration. Imagine not being able to catch a slip of a girl, as is our Lady Leighton. I should quite give up eating if such was the case."

"Lady Leighton? He chased your mother?" Mac-Dougal asked in horror.

"Leighton? Did I say Leighton? Hmm, meant Harlan, of course. How odd."

Duncan MacDougal looked at his friend and smiled. So that's how the wind blows, he thought.

"It's on behalf of Lady Harlan that I call on you for a favor," Leighton said. Blushing, he busied himself with his breakfast. Heaven and all the angels therein, help me, he thought in chagrin. I haven't blushed in twenty years.

MacDougal had been away, but could his friend of such masterly self-sufficiency be so changed as to actually require help? He arched an eyebrow and said, "I am at your service. What I can do for you?"

"As you know, I escorted Lady Harlan home last evening. The Prince frightened the lady with his advances. She climbed off a balcony and tore her dress and could not reappear in the ballroom. My reputation, unfortunately, does not allow me to be known as having helped her. I am not proud of the fact. It must not be known I was in her company alone. Can you imagine the speculation on the torn dress? You can see the predicament. She told her grandfather that you secured a carriage before you informed them she had returned home ill. You can see how serious the situation is. Would you be so kind as to call on her to see if she survives?"

"Her illness or her grandfather's wrath?" Duncan asked.

"Both."

"Yes, I am acquainted with Lord Stewart's wrath."

"You are? How so?" Ward asked.

" 'Tis a long time ago. It was when Evelyn ran off, leaving her daughter. Lord Harlan wasn't much of a husband, but he was devastated. Drank himself to death. Stewart is a hard man, I assure you, and trusts no one. I'm amazed he allowed his granddaughter to go off with the Prince. He must be getting senile, for it is my experience he watches everything."

"Exactly my sentiment, for I was horrified when she left the room on Prinny's arm. That's why I followed them. I could take action only surreptitiously."

"Why in heaven's name did you get involved?" MacDougal asked.

"I'm not sure. She seems so fragile and helpless, which I know not to be the case. Still, I found myself drawn in. I can't for the life of me see why. Why should I care about a silly girl? Perhaps I admire her spirit in overcoming her mother's scandal and don't want her to fail. Yes, I suppose that's it. I know only too well what an unsavory reputation can do. Mine is of my own making; hers was through no fault of her own."

"I would be most pleased to call on the young lady," Duncan said.

"I've brought a book. Will you give it to her?"

"Certainly, and a few posies would be in order, I should think."

"Duncan, you don't know how this relieves my mind. Do you suppose you could take her under your care? Keep a weather eye open, as it were. Lord Stewart is obviously an idiot. She has a swarm of suitors, so you'd not be singled out. It would mean a great deal to me. I would only bring undesirable speculation to her."

"Consider it done. Perhaps we could arrange for you to meet her on some occasions, quite by accident, to be sure," Duncan said cheerfully.

Leighton's jaw tightened. His attraction to the young lady was leading him beyond the bounds. Of what, though? Was Duncan's eagerness on behalf of his own interest in pursuing the charmer?

Perhaps he should have chosen a less attractive man to play protector. Whenever had he entertained jealousy? Damn, this was not to his liking.

MacDougal smiled at this revealing exchange. The man's besotted. "Why don't you directly declare interest? More than one rake has settled down with a fair maiden."

"I hadn't thought of it in that light. I don't know if I would make a decent husband or not. My life has not been devoted to that possibility."

"You're the first man I ever heard wonder whether he would make a good husband. It has been my experience that all men are sure they will. If not, what difference? I'm quite shocked."

"Duncan, you're bamming me."

"You deserve it. Well, I shall do as you ask. Give me the book. I'll pick up some posies and do the pretty for you," Duncan said, and laughed, which brought a snappy sparkle to his hazel eyes.

Now I've added bribery to my lies, Angel thought with growing horror. She was sure that hell's fires beckoned. Her old nanny had been correct in her strict warnings on sinful ways. A nunnery looks more appealing by the moment, she mused. Slowing her steps on the way to breakfast, she took a deep breath. As of this moment, I shall be the epitome of clearheaded thinking. Calm and proper decorum will be my motto. A sophisticated lady shall emerge and the schoolroom hoyden will disappear forever.

Quietly entering the room, she took her place at the table. Lord Stewart noted the pale, fragile complexion and shadowed eyes, and he felt a pang.

"Are you still unwell, my dear?" he asked.

"Not really, I just didn't sleep well. I realize my actions were very foolish. I just didn't think the

Prince would be so rude," she said, dropping her eyes with a delicate flutter.

Mary Beth, a study in gray with dainty lace collar and cuffs, narrowed her eyes in disbelief at Angel's blatant theatrical maneuvering.

Angel blushed. The image of Lord Leighton flashed in her mind, totally unbidden, and she shifted in discomfort.

Mary Beth pursed her lips.

The morning meal was eaten in silence. Lord Stewart rose to retire to his study. The ladies headed to the morning room, where Mary Beth intended to have a very serious discussion with her niece.

The hour was too early for callers, yet the butler announced the arrival of Major-General Mac-Dougal. Lord Stewart led the ladies into the salon, where he greeted the waiting gentleman.

"It is a great pleasure to see you once again. Especially so since you have rendered us a great service," Lord Stewart said.

Angel blushed. Mary Beth frowned.

MacDougal looked magnificent in his scarlet coat, clutching roses and a book.

"I was glad to be of service, I assure you," MacDougal replied. There was a tightness to his voice, different from his usual effusive manner. His eyes flickered as they moved past Mary Beth and came to focus on Lady Harlan.

"I come in hopes of finding you much improved," he said with a slight bow. "These are to cheer you up, and the book was intended to while away your hours as you convalesced. However, I am most gratified to find you in blooming health."

Angel thought she would die. Mayhap the shadows under my eyes show a little, she hoped.

She dropped him a curtsy and graciously accepted the gifts.

"Sir, you are too kind. I am better, and I do thank you for your help last evening. Please be seated. Can we offer you some coffee or tea?" Angel asked. Her heart was positively pounding in her chest.

MacDougal turned to Mary Beth as if he had not even heard Angel. "It is an unexpected pleasure to see you once more. I hope my intervention on behalf of your niece caused you no alarm," he smoothly said.

Mary Beth blushed.

Angel observed this with surprise and also noted her aunt's slight vexation. "Would you care for some coffee or tea?" Angel repeated.

"Eh, ah, coffee, er, no. I've come only to reassure myself that you were not seriously indisposed.

"I do appreciate your concern and again extend my thanks," Angel said, becoming aware of a sudden indescribable tension.

They all sat like birds on a fence while the conversation died. Finally, Lord Stewart spoke up, "You've been to India, I'm told. I daresay it must be a fascinating place."

"Indeed," MacDougal agreed.

Angel fidgeted with the flowers. Glancing at the book, she could see it was a collection of Christopher Marlowe's works, and her heart leapt. She pulled it closer to her lap and allowed the flowers to hide it. Her fingers moved along the soft leather binding. She knew, just knew, it was from Lord Leighton. An unexplained, glowing expression lit her face. It apparently was contagious, for Major-General MacDougal broke into a broad grin and his expressive eyes twinkled.

"Would you all join me for a night of opera? I am

anxious to renew old acquaintances and make new," he said, nodding toward Angel.

Mary Beth raised her hand to her lips with a quick intake of breath. She glanced at Angel, who was still watching the compelling MacDougal.

"How lovely. That is the one entertainment we have not had the pleasure of attending," Angel said in girlish delight. She looked to her aunt.

"Yes, that would be most diverting," Mary Beth said with breathless apprehension.

"Then it is settled. How would tomorrow evening suit?" he asked, looking at Angel, who nodded her approval. "I shall call for you at eight," he said, rising to take his leave. He bowed to both ladies and bade them good day.

They sat a moment in silence after his departure.

"Well, I never thought I'd have a major-general among my suitors," Angel said.

Mary Beth made no comment.

8

Dear Libby.

You will not believe what happened to me. I hesitate to tell you, but, of course, I shall. You must burn this letter as soon as you read it. I trust you to do so. Before I begin, I ease your mind that the tale ends rather well, although I am in disgrace with my family. At least temporarily, for I am sure I have placated them for the most part. The unfortunate thing is that I am a fool in Lord Leighton's eyes. That, I'm sure, is good news to you and everyone in my family, although they are not aware of that fact. All this is confusing, I am sure, so I shall explain.

Remember, you must burn this letter upon the first reading. No one must find it!

First of all, never trust the Prince of Wales. He is all affability and charm, but he chases one if one happens to find oneself alone with him, which unfortunately I did.

Do not admonish me; just don't go off with the Prince if he should wish to show you some *objet d'art.* I promise it will not be an edifying experience.

Believe me, a Season is full of unimaginable and unexpected traps.

At any rate, I unfortunately allowed the Prince
to escort me to see some silly statue of Venus by
some even sillier Renaissance sculptor. It was dis-
gusting! She was naked except for a drape that
didn't cover anything. He thought it beautiful and
that it resembled me. Well, she (the statue) had huge
hips. Now, Libby, I've gone through life with the dis-
advantage of being small, and that no one takes me
seriously. One has to be tall to be given credit. Being
blond, blue-eyed, and small has only allowed me to
be cute and stupid. Well, I am neither, as well you
know.

To get on with the story, the Prince chased me
around the table. I don't know if he intended to kiss
me or not. I was not inclined to find out. He was
in the midst of telling me something, when a
footman announced that Lord Leighton needed to
see him immediately. Then I heard footsteps and
thought he was returning. Terrified, as you can
imagine, I ran to the balcony outside the French
doors. I climbed off the balcony into a tree and
clung for dear life. Now, Libby, I can just see your
horrified expression, but what else was there to do?
The Prince is so old and fat! Surely, we can assume
no honorable intentions were present.

Fortunately, Lord Leighton had noticed the
Prince escort me to the gallery. So he went in search
of us and found me hanging in the tree. Oh, Libby,
my beautiful dress was ripped beyond redemption.
At any rate, Lord Leighton managed to get me out
of the tree. We hid in the bushes while some silly
fool proposed to an even sillier girl. I started to
giggle and Lord Leighton kissed me to shush me.
Libby, it was heavenly. Oh, I tell you, it is grand fun
to be kissed by someone who knows how. I have

never been kissed before, since Tommy Ashley
kissed me by the river, but then I was twelve and
he certainly didn't know how, being all of thirteen.
Besides, he did it on a dare from Bobby, so that
didn't count.

My dress was torn, so Lord Leighton covered me
with his evening cape and took me home. I had
rather thought he might kiss me again, but he did
not. He is divinely handsome. His reputation makes
him not acceptable, and I regret that.

Grandfather is furious and so is Mary Beth. I've
told a pack of lies and will probably burn in hell
for it. I shall have to be very careful henceforth.
Never trust anyone. Truly, you can get in the worse
predicaments by being naïve. Well, I am no longer
naïve and shall not go off with anyone again, prince
or no.

I realize now I must choose a husband. For the
life of me I can't think who it should be. They are
either old and lecherous, young and foolish, young
and poor, or old and poor. My, how I run on. Burn
the letter and, next, I shall write and tell you of
some proper bore that I have chosen to wed. You
may not believe it, but school is ever so much easier.

Love,
Angel

P.S. Grandfather does not know Lord Leighton
rescued me or that I climbed a tree.

Angel sealed the letter just as Mary Beth knocked
on her bedroom door. Thrusting the letter into her
secretary, she rose to cross the room. Mary Beth
entered with a scowling face. The expression was
contagious and Angel unwittingly answered it in
kind.

"You needn't frown at me, Angel. It is not I who
created the situation of last evening," Mary Beth

said, primly taking a seat as if she were about to take up residence.

Angel's spirits sagged, a lecture was to be forth-coming with too many questions.

"Now, tell me all that happened, and why," Mary Beth commanded with folded hands and a piqued expression.

Angel sighed. There was something penetrating about Mary Beth. One was not able to fob off just any tale and expect her to believe it.

"What is it you want to know?" Angel reluctantly and evasively asked.

"Only everything," Mary Beth said, and smiled a knowing smile.

Drat her, Angel thought. Only the truth would do, but she would not tell her about the kiss.

After listening to the account as it did indeed happen—without the kiss—Mary Beth rolled her eyes to heaven.

"Angel, there is nothing wrong in what you did. Actually, you extricated yourself from a dilemma that is best forgotten. I sincerely doubt the Prince has given any thought to your disappearance. If he has, be assured it is only to question what he might term your incredible shyness or lack of taste concerning fine art or captivating men. If, indeed, he has considered you at all, it will be that you are merely too soon from the schoolroom. You were correct in escaping. I just wish you had not done so via a tree."

Angel's eyes softened with relief. "You don't think me a ninny?"

"Heavens, no! I only wish your grandfather had controlled the situation to begin with, or that I had insisted on joining in the tour. I was so busy judging Father's lack of perception, I failed to react with dispatch. I apologize."

"Oh, Mary Beth, you're wonderful. Do you really think I am not such a fool? Oh, I hope Lord Leighton sees it that way," Angel said, hugging her aunt with enthusiasm.

A clouded expression crossed Mary Beth's eyes. So that's the way it is. May heaven help us.

"I'm sure he thinks you only made an unwise choice. However, why should you care what he thinks? He does not strike me as a man who carries tales," she asked in trepidation of the real reason.

Angel masked her expression, realizing she had revealed too much. "No reason of import, I just don't wish to seem silly in his eyes."

"He cannot be considered a suitor for your hand, Angel. He is far too well-known as the rake of a century. I doubt if Charles the Second had a greater success with the ladies." Sadness lingered in her words.

Angel looked questionably toward her aunt. A suitor? All the saints above, she thought, Leighton seeks no wife.

"I do not suppose that is even an idea we need to entertain. It is not likely that he would consider taking a wife, and certainly not me. So rest easy, but you cannot deny he is compelling," Angel softly replied.

"No, he is most compelling, as you say. That is the danger of him. Do be careful, love."

"He thinks of me as a green girl who needs to be saved from folly, nothing more. He is not in the petticoat line," Angel said. The regret in her voice was unmistakable.

Mary Beth sighed. She knew the pain of disappointment. "Let us put all this behind us. We have several invitations, and your come-out ball is but a week away. I must have your promise nothing will happen to spoil all we have accomplished," Mary Beth said.

Angel rose from the settee and twirled around. She faced her aunt with the most saintly expression imaginable. She dipped into a demure, obsequious, and graceful curtsy to end all curtsies. She smiled a gentle, shy, and beguiling smile, batted her lashes, and abruptly stood up. "Now, how was that?" she asked.

Mary Beth let out a gasp and burst into laughter. "You can do that?"

"Of course, and you believe it too," Angel bragged with a laughing toss of her head.

"You were meant for the stage. It is incredible," she said, still laughing. Immediately, she raised her hand and cautioned, "However, no stage!"

"Hmm, now that might be better than a nunnery," Angel said, placing her hands on her hips, swaying in a rather provocative manner.

"Angel, you will send me to an early grave. Keep the seraphic expression at all times. I can deal only with that," she said, still merrily laughing at her niece's antics.

"Aye, ducky," Angel replied with a wink and one last wiggle of her hips before the expression of pure virtue reappeared upon her face.

"You're incorrigible!"

As soon as Mary Beth departed, Angel sent Jeanne off to post the letter, then sat down to look at the lovely gilt-edged book of plays and poems. Carefully opening the leather cover, she read the inscription: "Angel Harlan, 'Clad in the beauty of a thousand stars . . .' Marlowe's Helen of Troy has a rival, and London a sprightly breath of spring air. This Angel has no wings, so flights to the treetops will remain a pleasant memory forever. WL."

Her fingers gently touched the handwritten words, and they lingered. No heart raced, no pulses pounded, only a quiet joy sprang in her soul. She would tuck the feeling safely away to savor when the nights seemed long and lonely. She could dance with a thousand partners and receive a million compliments, but none could match the tenderness of this. For now, that was enough. Would it remain so? She did not know.

9

The Duke of Albrion, Earl of Seaton, William Augustus Corners called upon Lady Harlan armed with a charming bouquet of spring flowers. One would have to look far and wide to find so attractive a man. His broad shoulders fitted the tailored blue superfine coat to perfection. He wore the usual buff pantaloons and flawlessly polished, high-top Hessians. While being dressed in the manner of every other aristocrat for day wear, he did more than justice to his tailor. It was bantered about that Weston would do well to furnish the duke's coats gratis as a proclamation to his talents. There was no denying his outstanding good looks. He handed the butler his walking stick and hat, and he was ushered into the blue salon.

The duke bowed to the ladies at his entrance and proceeded to cross the room. Angel watched his stately approach. He doesn't walk; he saunters with all the regality of a king, she thought.

"Good morning, Lady Harlan," he said, taking her hand and bowing over it with a light kiss of precise and proper pressure and length of duration.

"Good morning, Your Grace," she said with a

slight curtsy, for she had risen upon his noteworthy entrance. Somehow, she mused, one was compelled to do so. She smiled at the thought and looked straight to his broad chest. I wonder if I come up to his belly button? She blushed at so improper a thought.

"These flowers remind me of you," he said, presenting the token.

Great heavens, she thought, I remind yet another gentleman of something or other. "How perfectly charming of you," she said, her eyes twinkling in direct contrast to her demure countenance.

Albrion did not notice. He turned to Mary Beth, "I am gratified to find you both in the bloom of good health."

Taking a seat, he crossed his muscular legs and brushed off some imaginary speck of lint. "I heard you became ill during the Prince's reception. I do hope and certainly surmise you are feeling all the thing this morning."

Angel cast a wary look toward Mary Beth.

"A mere trifling, to be sure. It is easy to suffer from the oppressive heat of the Prince's gatherings," Mary Beth smoothly replied.

Angel cast another glance, but this time it was amusement. Her aunt never ceased to amaze her. She could probably lie her way out of hell, Angel thought. It must be a family trait.

"May we offer you some refreshment?" Mary Beth asked.

"No, thank you. I have come to ask you both to attend the opera with me this evening." He would remain the fifteen or twenty minutes deemed appropriate for a morning call unless previously arranged. This was not a conscious thought, only years of conditioning. The duke was a paragon of the proper manners so necessary for social compliance.

"How kind of you, but we are engaged to attend with Major-General MacDougal," Angel replied.

The duke's handsome countenance actually took on a crestfallen look.

"Do join us," Mary Beth hastily interjected. "It would please us to have you, and how nice to even the numbers."

He could hardly cry off, so, of course, he said he would be delighted to join the party. Is the Scotsman a suitor also? he wondered. If so, he is definitely competition. A fleeting pang of jealousy clouded his fine brown eyes. No, it was hardly likely that Lady Harlan would choose a Scotsman. The English are far superior, he thought. This incredible idea gave him comfort, and a devastating smile lit his face.

"I am honored," he said, rising to take his leave. The time was set and he bowed to the ladies. Taking Angel's hand once more, he looked into her shimmering eyes. "Until tonight."

The ladies sat down in silence directly upon his departure.

"Well, I think you have a worthy suitor," Mary Beth said finally.

"Yes, indubitably worthy. He is frightfully handsome and his manners are perfection itself. He would be the catch of the Season, to be sure," Angel replied. He is handsome, Angel thought, and very pleasant. One could do worse. She wondered why she wasn't elated by the idea.

"Do you think him suitable—rather, do you like him?"

"Of course I like him. What is there to dislike? He is most agreeable," Angel answered.

"I hate the word 'agreeable.' It's like fine or nice.

Lacks any character, don't you agree?" Mary Beth said.

Angel burst into laughter. "You're so serious. I like him, I think he's fine and agreeable. Do the three add up to a bit more commitment?"

Mary Beth smiled. "I know who will approve," she teased with a hint of warning not lost on Angel.

"Who?"

"Your grandfather."

They both fell silent.

Time had flown. Anticipation usually brought the dragging of hours, but this evening had arrived before she had time to assess it. Grandfather more than approves, she knew. In fact, he bordered on being obnoxious about the invitation. She was traversing along a path that had diminishing options of direction.

Angel did like the duke, or what she knew about him. It was difficult to discern a true sense of the man. Perhaps during this evening she would get to know him better. That was obvious enough, but rather she should like a greater understanding of him. He seemed somehow to not be real . . . How odd, she thought.

Jeanne bustled about, happily arranging Angel's coiffure and exclaiming how becoming the arrangement of Greek-style curls were. Angel took a cursory look and shrugged her shoulders.

Next, Jeanne slipped the gown of embroidered white silk thread on the finest muslin over Angel's arms. The neckline was low and square-cut. The sleeves were caught up on the outer arm, giving a classical drape. The folds of her skirt draped from under the bosom and gave length of line to the petite figure.

Mary Beth slipped into the room just as Jeanne

had finished her mistress's toilette. "You look lovely, dear," she exclaimed. Mary Beth wore a soft dove-gray silk dress trimmed with lustrous blond lace.

"Mary Beth, you look wonderful," Angel lied, wishing her aunt would try a bolder style of dressing. She allowed herself to look ten years older than she was.

"Ah, I hear your censure. However, we are not marrying me off, and I thank the Lord for that blessing," Mary Beth said, tiny dimples peeking out at the corners of her mouth.

"Blessing, indeed, you could not be more correct," Angel said as she picked up her reticule and fan.

Jeanne decided she would never understand the gentry. Her mistress looked like the angel she was, yet she stood there whining. Dropping a curtsy, she left the room muttering, "They're never satisfied."

Major-General MacDougal stood with the Duke of Albrion at the foot of the sweeping staircase. He was a full head shorter than the duke, but no less impressive in his scarlet coat. His animation and vitality were as unconscious a part of him as was his military bearing. By contrast, the duke looked marvelously handsome because of his classic features and sartorial elegance, but no personality was perceivably visible.

The ride to Covent Garden Opera House was unremarkable. The conversation consisted of generalities. Once inside, Angel's youthful enthusiasm surfaced with an engaging sparkle in her spectacular eyes. The great duke was pleased and amused. He sent her an understanding smile that quite took her by surprise.

The soaring music of love's betrayal and tragedy filled Angel with bittersweet emotion, as is the wont

of most operas. Her eyes became even more luminous and she fought back tears during the death
scene. Albrion made every effort to concentrate, but
shifted twice in his chair and even went so far as
to cover a revealing yawn. MacDougal spent the
evening surreptitiously glancing toward Mary Beth,
who kept her eyes stoically upon the stage.

During the return ride, all agreed that it was an
outstanding performance. All continued to cover
their thoughts with banal conversation. The tension
of hidden emotions crackled in the air with no
acknowledgment by the passengers. Their safety lay
in the assumed roles each chose to play.

"Lady Harlan, I am grateful for this evening with
you. Would you care to ride out with me on the
morrow?" the duke asked when they at last arrived
home.

Angel felt the net closing in. The death knell
tolled, and yet she nodded. "I would like that above
all else," she heard herself reply. It was as if
someone else answered for her.

Mary Beth blithely bade both gentlemen good
evening and turned to climb the stairs. Angel
scampered after her.

"You have made another conquest, I should say,"
Mary Beth said as they traversed the long corridor.

"Do you think so?" Angel asked with a flat voice.

Mary Beth sent a sensitive, questioning look to
her niece. "Indeed, I do. The duke is obviously
interested or he would not choose to ride with you
tomorrow for all the world to see."

"Yes, I suppose so. Well, good night, dear Aunt,"
she said, placing a kiss on her cheek.

Angel wore a conversation bonnet that had one
side of its brim coquettishly turned back, the other
primly pointed forward to hide the cheek. Lined

with pink rushing with matching ribbons that tied under the chin, it also sported a cluster of roses. Framing the face, thus making her eyes appear enormous, it could only be described as capable of weakening any man's resolve to remain single. All ladies knew the power of such hats and, of course, never let the male gender in on the secret.

She wore a pink spencer over her muslin gown. Ruffles decorated her neck and sleeves. Therefore, Lady Harlan appeared enchantingly feminine, and with her diminutive size, any red-blooded male would be overcome with the desire to protect and capture. Such was the wisdom of the ladies of her era who could only obtain status through marriage.

The effort was not lost upon the duke as he assisted Angel into the carriage. He smiled with genuine pleasure at being in her company. She appropriately dropped her eyes with a flutter, then smiled to herself as he climbed in next to her. She must tell Libby how easy it is to flirt when one seriously puts one's mind to it.

They covered the usual conversations on the weather, the congestion of the streets, and the health of family members.

Entering the park, they were seen by many members of society, who genteelly nodded. She was sure the fact that she sat by the duke's side would be common knowledge before she returned home. It is unfortunate the postal systems could not apply such efficiency, she wryly thought.

On several occasions Albrion pulled in his reins to speak with some friend or other. Angel continued in her practiced role of smiling prettily and offering few comments, and then only to agree. She was convinced her face would remain in the same expression for days, unable to return to an occasional frown.

The duke courted her with manners of interest and concern for her comfort. Was she too warm? If not, too chilly? When he got around to "Would you care to return?" she said yes.

So the outing, in the duke's eyes, was a resounding success. The *belle incomparable* was a delightful companion. She was very wise, for she had enough understanding to think him entirely correct upon his various observations. He liked intelligent ladies. Intelligent by his estimation meant agreement, and she was clearly just such a creature.

10

The Neoclassical Revival, which flourished in the last decades of the eighteenth century and the first of the nineteenth, was expressed in the houses, furnishings, and clothes of the wealthy. The birth of the revival began with the discovery of Pompeii and was reinforced by the republican thoughts that swept France. The final impetus was created with Napoleon's expeditions to Italy and the booty returned to France of the glories of Rome. It promoted the classical virtues of proportion, line, and the totality of design without unnecessary embellishment.

The fashionable world looked to ancient Greece and Rome for inspiration. Roman dress and coiffure became the rage. The Empire fashion, as it was known, is the small woman's dream come true. It flattered the small frame, seemingly by giving height, the slender by accentuating the lean line, and the graceful by enhancing fluid movement.

Joséphine Napoleon had shocked the world with the dampening of her petticoat, thereby causing the lightweight fabrics to cling to the body with movement. It was meant to produce the accentuating folds of ancient statues. The ideal body-revealing dress was achieved by hip-length boned stays. Drawers were sometimes preferred to the layers of petticoats.

Lady Harlan made her come-out in a cloud of French silk chiffon fashioned Empire gown of exquisite design. She wore no dampened petticoats, stays, or drawers; these artifices were left to the more worldly women or those in need of the enhancement of stays.

Her high-waisted bodice was beaded with pearls, as was the hem of her skirt and train. The sleeves were short and the modest décolletage revealed her feminine figure. Her classical coiffure of coils and ringlets was encircled with a leaf band of silver filigree, encrusted with pearls and diamonds. She might have been Livia having stepped from a carved panel of the Ara Pacis. No royal princess ever looked more regal, pampered, or self-assured. Her cheeks were lightly flushed and her heart fluttered in nervous anticipation, but these were not visible to the assembled guests.

A sweet-smelling profusion of white roses and silver ribbons bedecked the ballroom. Hundreds of candles glowed in the crystal chandeliers, which reflected a thousand fold in the gold Louis XIV mirrors. The polished white marble floor and illusionary ceiling paintings of mythical gods romping in the heavens created the ethereal background Lord Stewart wanted for Angel's ball.

He was indicating to everyone that he was presenting his beloved granddaughter, who could walk among royalty as if she had only deigned to come down from Mount Olympus. If one did not agree with him, then that was their want of intelligence.

She had surpassed his fondest wishes ever since

the incident on the night of the Prince's reception. True to her vow, Angel had moved through the demanding social events with serene demeanor and queenly graciousness. No one could refute she was the Seasons *belle incomparable*. She had won her place in society as the fragile beauty who could choose whomever she desired.

Speculation ran rampant on who the gentleman might be. Lady Harlan gave no inkling of partiality to any suitor. She treated her beaux with sparkling generosity and equal kindness.

Angel herself had no idea whom she might choose. Tonight, she carried Lord Hatton's gift of flowers as a token to his constant attention. Somehow, she thought she owed him that compliment, for his devotion never seemed to falter and he was always "there."

Lord Hatton's heart swelled with pride at the sight of the nosegay she carried. He knew she offered no more attention to him than any other young man, but this sign sent a momentary surge of hope in his quest to win the lady. He sighed at the thought with a sudden, inexplicable twinge of doubt. Lately, his pursuit had become less exciting, now that his father had come around. In fact, now that Lady Harlan was considered the catch of the Season, Hatton was beginning to resent his father's pressing of the matter, knowing full well the size of her dowry was the old man's reason, since society no longer held Lady Harlan responsible for her mother's scandal. Hatton moved among the guests with a vague and distracted expression.

Among the glittering guests stood the sartorially splendid Duke of Albrion, who watched Lady Harlan move onto the ballroom floor on the arm of her grandfather for the opening dance. His eyes were rich brown with flecks of gold and unusually glowed with warmth. Tonight, acute awareness gleamed in his keen eyes as he followed her movements.

He had openly joined the ranks of suitors by escorting her to the opera and driving through Hyde Park with her. He had purposefully danced at least one dance at each ball in which they met. This was duly noted and much discussed among the tabbies of the *ton*, some with relish, others with disdain and disappointed hopes for marriageable daughters.

Corners admired Lady Harlan's countenance and the courage with which she overcame the past family scandal. She had mettle, or she could not have erased the *beau monde* memory so handily.

Admiring her beauty, Lord Albrion acknowledged she would make a worthy duchess. He might wish she were taller, less fragile-looking, and a bit more robust. He considered her childbearing abilities. She was slender in hip and he realized that must be taken into consideration.

Languidly raising his eyeglass, he knew perfectly well a more lusty type of woman stirred his passion. Still, she was appealing enough for a wife. Lust, at any rate, should be left outside a marriage, he mused, smiling slyly at his observation.

Enough gathering moss, Lord Corners thought, putting his musings aside as he requested the next dance with the Duke of Devon's daughter. She blushed and tittered the whole tiresome time. Bored beyond measure, he used his considerable charm on the milk-and-water miss, since his duty was to do the pretty with as many young ladies as possible. It was expected of him, and he simply could not disappoint these hopeful ladies or their mothers. His ego did not suffer with the response he generally evoked, and he had grown accustomed to the worshiping glances of the hopeful young ladies. He heroically stifled a yawn.

After returning the Devons' daughter to her mother, he sought out Lady Harlan to honor with a dance. Lord Corners crossed the room just as the dowager Duchess of de Aubrey entered. The proper term of "dowager" brought a wicked gleam to his fine eyes, for while that was indeed the widow's position, the lady was exotically young and beautiful.

An epic response of gasps, turned eyes, and paused speech afflicted many guests, especially the male gender. The spectacular duchess was making her first public appearance following her period of mourning for the dear, old duke.

She was elegantly tall, raven-haired, and enormously wealthy. She appropriately wore lavender, which made her violet eyes scintillating beacons. The gown, though modestly cut, revealed her voluptuous breasts and creamy shoulders.

Lord Tutwiller clutched his chest. The ancient relic of a roué feared his heart might not withstand the sight of such a sublime lady. He clicked his tongue against his ill-fitting ivories and decried Father Time.

At the sight of the duchess, a sense of panic seized Lord Corners. He was a man of considerable sexual appetite carefully hidden from, and totally unknown by, the *haut ton*. He sincerely believed that one did *not* flaunt one's virility, especially if one was a true aristocratic genetleman, therefore he always kept his ladybirds sequestered. This was exactly the reason why he hated men such as the Marquess of Kendall, who showed insulting indifference to the capricious sensibilities of the *ton*.

Corners tore his eyes away from this enchantress, vowing to approach her at a more discreet time. He was sure that since the death of her elderly husband, she was in desperate need of a virile man. He intended to fulfill that need. Moving sharply away, lest his body give him away, he turned his attention in seeking out Lady Harlan.

Bowing over her hand, he looked into the cool, detached eyes. He watched the smile that did not reach her eyes when she nodded agreement. This took him quite by surprise. Never had he experienced anything but enthusiastic rapture at his request for anything, let alone a dance. Her attitude annoyed him.

"You look like a fairy princess this evening, Lady Harlan," Lord Corners said in silky tones, designed to flatter.

Angel bestowed a weak smile and said, "Thank you, your grace." She couldn't understand her lack of propensity to offer the expected enthusiasm to his compliment. To her horror, she wondered if she were becoming jaded. Up until this very moment, she thought only middle-aged men did that. A look of consternation crossed her face.

This sent the great duke into a panic. He raised his efforts to please. He charmed with practiced wit until he captured a genuine laugh from the elusive lady. Rewarded, he relaxed. For a few terrible moments, he considered the unlikely prospect of having lost his touch. What a shocking idea, he thought. Her smiling response restored his heretofore undisturbed ego.

Angel knew many eyes were upon them and she studied the duke for a moment. He smiled. He was attractive and charming without doubt, and she should consider him as a possible husband. She wondered just how easy that would be. He had managed to escape the petticoat line thus far. Her musing brought an enticing smile to her lips.

"Tell me, what brings that enchanting smile to your face and eyes? It is not me, for I have spent the entire time inveigling a single laugh from you," he said, breaking into her reverie.

"You would think it silly, your grace," she replied.

"Nothing that could bring such a smile could be anything but fascinating," he answered, feeling quite gallant.

"I was thinking of society smiles and manners and what really lies behind them," she answered, suddenly curious about his possible answer.

He stiffened a split second, then softly laughed. "I daresay we might find ourselves far less flattered," he said truthfully.

Angel laughed, liking his frank answer. "Your grace is correct and it is well to remember that, lest one come to believe so many pretty words."

"I should imagine in your case, you could safely take them to heart."

"Heavens, no! I should become unbearably proud and no one could ever match what is often passed as truth. Do you not think most of the compliments bestowed upon me should be given directly to my dowry?" she asked.

Quite shocked, he studied her a moment. The gleam of rancor in her eyes increased his interest. "One ought to know one's worth," he said quietly.

"Ah, but that's the fallacy, you see. Can one's own judgment be relied upon?" she said, sending him a coy dimpling smile.

The duke could think of no immediate reply. What an odd idea, he thought. He believed in his immeasurable worth with no fault to be found in his personality. He knew most people did not understand or, in fact, merit much praise.

"Perhaps, in most cases you are correct. Indeed, I believe you are," he said solemnly.

There was no way to pursue the topic, for the set ended. As the duke escorted her from the dance floor, his eyes again traveled to the Duchess of de Aubrey.

The spectacular lady was in deep conversation with that rake, Leighton. Corners' jaw muscles tightened. Angel's gaze followed his, and she was taken aback by the stab of pain in her breast.

"A handsome pair, to be sure," she said aloud with a snap of her fan in a flourish of motion.

"Er, yes," he said, continuing to gaze at the outstanding couple. Recovering himself, he bowed. "Thank you for the dance. I shall claim another, perhaps the dinner dance?"

"You do me honor, your grace," she dully answered.

The duke did not notice the dispirited note in her voice and moved quickly from her side.

Lord Hatton suddenly sprang before her with a flourishing bow. "Do me the honor for this dance," he beseeched.

"Why, Lord Hatton, I have been hoping to catch sight of you. You sweet dear. Thank you for these lovely flowers. You are too kind. Would you consent to sit with me during this set? I am breathless. I promise another later," she said in a honey-ladened voice.

Lord Hatton, who had been struggling on the fringes of her swains for weeks, considered this as yet another decided mark of distinction. He had never seen her sit with a gentleman during a ball. As he eagerly took a seat next to her, his earlier ambiguity faded with the power of her blue eyes and winsome smile.

"I'm thirsty. Aren't you? In fact, I'm quite parched," she said.

Puffed up with his obvious success, Lord Hatton happily excused himself to find the refreshment room and procure some punch.

Angel sat toying with her fan, not listening to the chatter of those clustered around her, when her eyes fell on Mary Beth gliding by in the arms of her partner, Major-General MacDougal. She had not noticed Mary Beth's departure from the edge of the dance floor. Mercy me, will wonders never cease? she mused. Mary Beth looked decidedly pleased and her cheeks glowed with a soft blush. It must be the heat, Angel thought as she continued to stare.

A creepy feeling of being watched took hold and she turned to find Lord Leighton, eyes fixed upon her, resolutely coming toward her. Delight sprang to her face in the form of a brilliant smile.

It almost stopped Ward in his tracks, his pulses leapt. Great Scott, he thought, what is happening to me? What powers does she hold? He continued toward her, the proverbial moth to the fire. With a wry humor, he smiled. It was usually considered the opposite in his romances.

He stretched out his hand and she rose, placing hers in his. He placed her hand on his arm and escorted her to the forming set.

"I should not have succumbed to the irresistible urge to ask for a dance," he said, "but as you see, I could not resist the temptation of an angel."

"Well, I should hope not. I doubt I would be having a come-out ball if it were not for you. I owe you a great debt."

"It is I who owe you," he said.

Angel looked into his lively blue-green eyes. She

was enchanted by the way they crinkled around the corners. That usually denoted humor, and so it was with Leighton, for he radiated an amused sense of the ridiculous. True, it often seemed to be wry, but always engaging.

"I believe it will not be ruinous to your reputation if I dance one dance with you during your honoring ball," Ward said.

"Is that why you never approach me on any other occasion?"

"Of course, we must see that no touch of 'unscrupulous' company taint your unblemished Season."

Angel laughed. "Thanks to you."

"Ah, but they were mere silly mishaps. I fear I present a far greater danger. Once, however, should do you no harm," he said. His smile was devastating.

"I shall be the judge of that," she teased.

"Unfortunately not. However, this brief moment will have to do. It gratifies me to see you such a success. Who shall be the lucky gentleman?"

"You mean the poor misguided soul that must keep me in check?"

"Ah, you were paying attention. Yes, who has the inside track?"

"I really don't know. There is a dearth of interesting possibilities. I am seriously considering joining a convent."

"Never do. You'd raise havoc in ecclesiastical circles. No, it must be some poor soul you can lead around."

"You think you know me well enough to choose? Then do so."

He laughed. "I'll keep it in mind, I promise."

"Do not spend much time in such thought. I'm sure I'd abhor anyone you might choose."

"You wound me! I, who know the whims of society, could choose a veritable paragon accepted by one and all."

"That, my lord, is exactly what I fear most."

"Indeed? You surprise me. I should have thought you would want a man of the highest distinction," he said in mock horror.

"You know exactly what I mean," she said, smiling with delight.

"I plead ignorance."

"Well, if he were a perfect paragon, think how tiresome that would be. I should have to be on my best behavior at all times."

"Hmm, I see your point. Then I shall choose one for you who will worship at your feet and think everything you do is wonderful. Now, how is that?" he asked.

"No, there are dozens that worship at my feet, or so they say, and I heartily suspect that fact," she said, laughing with a toss of her head.

He regarded her a moment. His heart constricted in his chest and he restrained himself from pulling her to him and covering her with kisses.

Suddenly the mood between them changed from playful banter to something else, something uncomfortable. The tension became awareness of the most compelling of emotions: desire.

The dying strains of the music temporarily ended Ward's misery. His expressive eyes became passive as if shuttered against a coming storm. Briskly escorting her back, he bowed.

"Take care, there are some places where angels dare not tread," he whispered.

She turned to look him directly in the eyes and saw only sadness. "Angels do not see evil in all things."

He was stunned by her perception. She may

be impulsive on occasion, but she was no child.

She watched him weave his way among the pressing throng and disappear among the guests.

11

Dear Libby,

My come-out ball was a resounding success. The ballroom was transformed into a veritable garden of white roses. The setting was all that Grandfather wished, and he looked like a peacock all puffed up with pride. I think, at last, I have given him what he wanted most: a way to lay to rest my impetuous mother's scandal forever.

I behaved exactly as he had always hoped I would. Are you quite surprised? Well, 'tis true; I am the paragon of a charming, mealymouthed miss. It is totally surprisng that such banal manners constitute what is considered admirable.

Doesn't it make more sense to admire someone for their intelligence, kindness, or wit? But, no, presenting oneself as an ignorant, helpless, modest, and innocent maid is what we are told a gentleman prefers in a wife. Why would a man want a simpering miss? For the life of me I can't figure it out. Can you imagine living with someone who can claim only the desired accomplishments of needlepoint, watercolors, or competence on the pianoforte? Boggles the mind. Why wouldn't a

gentleman want a lady with whom he could converse?
The Earl of Albrion has called several times. As for paragons, he is unsurpassed. I am to ride out with him shortly, and he is to escort me to the Duchess of Norfolk's ball. I find many of my suitors have departed the scene since the arrival of the great duke. He must be interested, or he would not have singled me out for all the world to see; still I do not sense any devotion. Time will reveal all, I suppose.

I danced once with Lord Leighton at my ball.

Love to you,
Angel

She rose from her desk and slipped into the jacket of her blue riding habit. Placing a saucy hat on her head, she smiled. The pale feathers curled along her cheek, giving a delightful, rakish look. There is nothing like a new bonnet to lift one's spirits, she mused before turning her steps to greet the awaiting duke.

Lord Corners rose when she entered the salon. He wore a brown riding jacket that fitted his broad shoulders snugly yet gave room for movement. The rich brown enhanced his warm brown eyes. He is mighty handsome, Angel thought as she crossed the room.

Smiling down to her, he said, "The day is that one day which comes in late May. The one where you could ride forever and admire the beauty of the world."

"Lord Corners, you have a poetic soul," she said with an approving note to her voice.

"Never considered that before, but you shall see. I doubt you'll wish to hurry home. Come, let us enjoy this magnificent day."

They did just that. It was a glorious day. One would have to be dead and buried to not feel the elation of such beautiful weather. It affected their conversation and the joy spread to their faces with smiles and harmony.

Though his matched pair were considered "sweet goers," he held them to a modest pace. Lord Corners greeted various friends and took care to introduce Angel. Her spirits were so full of the wonderful day, they translated into sparkling animation.

Lord Corners watched her gather in admiring glances and approval with satisfaction. He was correct; she would make him an admirable duchess. He felt a growing contentment with the idea. It was time to make his choice and set up his nursery, for his mother had begun to press him on the matter. There was a slight resistance to choice of Lady Harlan, but he could smooth those waters. He would invite Angel to meet his mother to overcome any doubt of suitability his mother harbored.

"Lady Harlan, I should be honored if you and your aunt would come down to Marlefort for a visit. I am anxious for you to meet my mother," he said with deceiving casualness.

Angel glanced sharply toward the duke. She knew such a visit was for inspection and subsequent approval or disapproval. The idea sent her heart tumbling, and a chill of apprehension shivered down her spine. This Season was devoted to the precise purpose of catching a husband. That now seemed at hand, and she faltered in her resolve.

"How lovely," she said quietly at her pulse pounded in her temples.

"It will be but a month before our friends scatter to their estates, or perhaps Bath, to escape the summer heat. I should hope you might come in a fortnight. Will your grandfather consent?"

How innocent the question sounded, she thought, but it was paramount to the acceptance of her likely engagement to the duke. She could not answer immediately, caught by the overwhelming implications.

"Lady Harlan . . . or may I call you Angel?" he asked.

"Of course," she replied.

"Then please call me William," he said magnanimously, as if he were giving a great gift. Indeed he was, for such intimacy was bestowed on only a few deserving souls. She turned to look at him and he returned a gentle, understanding smile. "Do not be afraid. I admire your reticence, it is seemly. Do consider a visit. It will be no more than that, if you should choose to view it as such. I will not press you; however, I want you to meet my mother."

"I will be delighted to visit your country estates. I much prefer country living, my lord," she replied.

"Indeed? I do not. I do spend the summer at Marlefort, but time passes heavily. With you there, I am sure it will be just as delightful as this day."

Angel could not summon a reply. Her world was closing in. She had directed her steps to this moment, and it brought none of the pleasure she had expected. She stole another peek of the duke; he seemed kind enough, but there was an arrogance expressed as part of his inherited right. She was positive he wasn't even aware of it.

Conversation ceased when Corners turned sharply and raised his hand in an effusive greeting to Lord Leighton, who approached riding next to the glamorous Duchess of de Aubrey. She looked positively splendid. Her beauty was rich and warm.

She emanated all the womanly attributes of an Aphrodite.

"Good day, Lady de Aubrey and Lord Leighton," Corners said, never taking his eyes off the lady, who sat elegantly sidesaddle on a beautiful chestnut horse.

While exchanging greetings, Angel felt Lord Leighton's eyes resting on her. She leveled her eyes to his and saw a sadness in them. A penetrating shock reverberated through her body, and tiny tears forced their way to the corners of her eyes. She squared her shoulders and fought them back.

Lord Leighton's lips gave hint of a beginning smile, which faded almost instantly before he nodded to her. She looked away. Oh, my, she thought, the man moves me. I cannot help it. Simply to see him brings out the most uncomfortable and powerful reactions. She dropped her eyes, knowing full well they revealed far too much.

The duchess allowed her gaze to rest briefly upon the slender, ethereal young lady, and she smiled. She sensed the pain in Lady Harlan, and her heart went out to the child. I know only too well her position, she thought, and was saddened by the idea.

The Duke of Albrion hid his own reaction. The magnificent woman before him brought out a stirring passion that set his blood afire.

"I have just invited Lady Harlan to join me at Marlefort in two weeks' time. I am getting up a weekend party before we all scatter to various summer residences. I should be delighted if you both would join me," the duke heard himself say. He was surprised as the words escaped his lips, but not as his body trembled with anticipation.

Angel turned to the duke in amazement. This

measurably changes the aspects of the weekend. Did he understand her reluctance and, in deference to her, offer the less intimate connotation of a weekend party. If so, he was more kind than she had supposed, which would certainly bode well if she married him.

Lord Leighton was equally amazed, for Corners hated him. His eyes narrowed and traveled from Angel to the duke, then to the lovely duchess. He began to understand and his spirits lifted to a new hope. Time could only be his ally.

The air crackled with hidden emotions and false words. Society training disguised well their ulterior motives, some known and some unknown.

"What a splendid idea. A quiet weekend among friends is precisely what would please me most," the duchess replied. The accent on the word "friends" was offered wryly, for she hardly knew the Duke of Albrion.

Angel took the meaning to be the duchess's opportunity to be with Lord Leighton, and her spirits sagged in utter desolation.

The duke took the meaning as the duchess's interest in himself, and he smiled with satisfaction.

Leighton felt dismay, just as Angel did, but his stemmed from the possible pain gathering on the horizon like summer clouds before a storm. If Lady Harlan felt a *tendre* for Corners, there was certain hurt, and as for himself, it would be nothing short of hell to be so near and keep his distance.

All these thoughts were hidden behind elegant manners and small talk. Their parting was full of smiling faces and enthusiastic comments on the anticipation for the upcoming weekend.

Lord Corners set the curricle in motion and they continued their outing. For Angel the enjoyment faded, and she sat quietly listening to the duke. He applied himself to general, lighthearted conversation, but the rapport between them never returned. The polite distance of two acquaintances filled its place.

Angel was grateful no one was home to question her on the outing. She went directly to her room. Closing the door, she leaned against it, as if to hold the world at bay. Thoughts and emotions were crowding into her mind, all demanding attention. Removing her charming hat and jacket, she caught her reflection. A dry, pinched look of dissatisfaction stared back. She was not actress enough to remove it, and since she was alone, she would indulge it.

Why this wild uneasiness? She knew full well Lord Leighton was far too dangerous for her to be seen with, yet she was becoming absorbed in his presence. His being well-favored had nothing to do with it. The duke was more so. What was it that set her heart racing? There was an inner magic he radiated. Why did she know she would never tire of life with him? What made her so sure there was a deep and profound side to him?

By contrast, she clearly understood what life would be with the duke. In her innocence, she was wrong, of course, but she had the perception to sense the shallowness in him. The hidden aspects of the duke were worrisome. No such feeling, idea, or thought could she attach to Leighton.

I cannot consider Leighton. He has said as much. But why not? A small voice whispered in her mind: Because he does not wish it. He speaks of his reputation but not of his change. He says he cannot champion me, but it must be that he does not wish to do so. There is your answer, she told herself. He would change it if he chose to do so. Yes, he thought her attractive and had taken pity on her. Pity! What an unpalatable word.

She wept. Her future was almost assured. She would meet the Dowager Duchess of Albrion and win her over. You silly goose, she admonished herself, and wept more. I should be grateful, the duke is all kindness and would make a good husband. A slightly detached husband, but that was what she had claimed to want. Now that it was about happen, she stood trembling with reluctance, because a gentleman with compelling blue-green eyes had showed something else. How foolish I am. Few can hope for any more than what is about to be offered to me. This last thought offered no comfort.

12

Madeleine de Aubrey rose from the pianoforte and cheerfully greeted the Marquess of Kendall.

"Leighton, what a pleasant surprise! What prompts such an early call?" she asked, moving from the bench to offer her hand. "Please be seated," she said with a gesture of her slender white hand.

She moved gracefully to take a seat on an exquisite Louis XVI divan in the style of Sené and Jacob. Its blue-and-white paintwork and silk liseré fabric surrounded her with elegance as if in tribute to the lady herself. She folded her hands and waited for him to speak.

Leighton lounged back, crossed his legs, and appeared to study the toe of his Hessian boot.

"Am I to comment on the superb shine you have managed to obtain?" she asked with a teasing smile.

He returned her smile. "No, I wish to discuss an awkward subject and find myself at a loss for words."

Madeleine de Aubrey rested her velvety eyes on Leighton's face and noted the troubled lines about his mouth and eyes. She sat back. An aura of serenity and kindness shone from her eyes as if to say, I understand.

"Pray, say it. Do not be concerned that I should receive your words in anything but friendship."

A tentative smile hovered a second on his lips. "As you know, we are invited to the Duke of Albrion's weekend party. I find that request singularly surprising, for he cannot abide me."

A knowing smile materialized. "You must surely know he wants my presence, not yours. You will provide the decoy he deems necessary."

"I thought as much, and I do not like it."

A silvery laugh of charming proportions escaped her lips. "You flatter me. Now, I shall also be equally as frank. I have spent the last seven years with a husband who made my life a misery. No man will ever hold the power to do so again. If I should fix a *tendre* on a gentleman, it will be from the knowledge that he loves me and not my physical appearance or my fortune."

This time, her melodious laugh carried an edge of rancor. "Ward, we unfortunately attract the opposite sex for the wrong reasons. Don't ask me why, but there it is. You need not concern yourself for me. I shall effortlessly hold the lustful duke at bay."

"If you prefer not to go, we can decline," he said with a note of reluctance. His own unknown destiny prompted him with the nagging need to attend.

"I think we can turn the ruse of my presence against the duke and to our advantage. If I am not mistaken, you are taken by the charming Lady Harlan."

"Am I that obvious?"

"Perhaps not to all. However, it was obvious to me. I will gladly help you."

"That is the dilemma. You know very well, a lady

seen too often in my company is assumed to be my mistress. I do not wish to bring, unwittingly, any offensive speculation or gossip about you."

"Ward, you are the most honorable man I know."

He scoffed. "Honorable, no. I am thinking of the inevitable implications, and they must be considered regardless of my wish in hopes—"

"In hopes of winning the lady for your own?"

"I'm afraid that is impossible. But I know, without doubt, he will bring her sorrow."

"Then it is settled, we go. I need some excitement in my life. Now, what is it you wish me to do?"

"Could you test Corners' faithfulness, the sincerity of his commitment to Lady Harlan? Although I do not think it a true test. You could charm the birds from the trees. I doubt Corners could resist you."

"Are they betrothed?"

"Not yet, but I am sure that possibility is not far in the future."

"Ward, are you forgetting Lady Harlan? What of her? What does she wish?"

Ward sat a moment unable to answer. Finally he said, "I do not know. Above all else, I wish for her happiness."

"If I bewitch Lord Corners, which anyone wearing a skirt and holding passable good looks could easily accomplish, in order to show his perfidious nature, will your lovely young lady stand in shame and embarrassment? What if she desires the match? He *is* considered quite a catch."

"If she chooses him, I want her to know what kind of man he is."

"Ward! Now you are overstepping your rightful bounds. If you break off the budding romance, then you must be willing to declare yourself to her."

"Madeleine, just go for me. Let us see if the duke

can withstand your charms. Let him sink his own
ship."

"Ward, you devious man! I take back my compliment."

"What compliment?"

"The one where I said you are the most honorable
man I know."

"I told you, you were mistaken. Let us unmask
the lecher and hope for the best," he said.

"Think about your marked attachment to Lady
Harlan."

Next, Ward called upon Duncan MacDougal. He
was restless with mixed motives crowding his mind.
This state of affairs was disconcerting to a
gentleman who had managed to live life ordered to
his specifications. The impervious Lord Leighton
was touched at last by the events that usually affect
all men. He was at loose ends and so, now, he sat
discussing the invitation with Duncan.

"I cannot imagine his asking me for any other
reason except that by doing so, he could include
Madeleine de Aubrey.

Duncan watched his friend. Ward did not seem
downcast precisely, but bedeviled and restless.
Never had he seen this imperturbable man so
unsettled.

"I think he is openly wooing Angel Harlan and
lusting after Madeleine," Leighton explained with
utter disgust. "Can you imagine her future?"

"Whose?"

"Why, Lady Harlan's, of course," Ward replied
in surprise at his friend's lack of perception.

"What of the Duchess of de Aubrey?" Duncan
asked.

Ward was taken aback. "She told me she could

handle Lord Corners, and I assume she is correct."

"A rather large assumption. I should think she is the vulnerable one."

"How so?"

"Is she to be your next ladylove?" Duncan asked.

"Great heavens, man, no. She is a friend. I've only escorted her on a few occasions as she reenters society after her mourning."

"You say you don't, or can't, woo Lady Harlan because of this infamous reputation of yours; yet, what of the duchess's reputation? If, as you say, to be in your company constitutes almost criminal proportions just short of treason or some such fancy, how can you risk hers?"

"Duncan, you're hoaxing me."

"Hell, no, you talk gibberish, man. You're besotted. Your brain must be mush."

"Don't you see, I've lived my life without thought of society's petty censures."

"Aye, that cavalier attitude has now bound you as tightly as a shorn Samson."

Leighton's jaw muscle tightened. He admired Duncan's frankness, but the bald truth was not pleasant to hear.

"You said you would keep an eye on Lady Harlan. What is your opinion?" Ward asked.

"And so I have, as best I could. The duke has stepped in as the most likely suitor. I could only prevent that by declaring for her myself. While the lady has charm, I do not wish her for my wife. Nor do I wish to spoil an obvious suitable alliance for her. It just might be the one she wants."

"Haven't you been listening to me? Corners is a scoundrel. He'll treat her like chattel. Never could he be faithful to her. The damn hypocrite mouths pious prattle and exhibits an honorable facade, but he is more the rake than I could hope to be in a lifetime. Even in my finest moments and with my exaggerated reputation, I pale by comparison."

Duncan laughed. "I get the drift. Yet, you expect me to stay the engagement by escorting her to the opera? A feeble attempt at accomplishing what you really want. I could call the man out and deftly dispose of him," Duncan said with a wry smile.

Leighton smiled. Put into words, the situation sounded ridiculous.

"An outing to the opera is hardly heavy artillery, eh? Then you tell me how to manage this muddle."

"Declare for her yourself; otherwise, dismiss it."

"How can I?"

"I suppose you could say something like this: it may have come to your attention that my feelings for you have grown in such proportions that I can only be happy if you will do me the inordinate honor of accepting my beseeching plea to become my wife."

Leighton laughed. "You have it down rather pat. You ought to seek a wife."

"I may."

"Really? Who?"

"Never mind that. It is your courtship we are discussing."

"I'm not sure I could make her happy. There is my past, and her family's approval is unlikely."

"So, you quit the field and allow someone else who is capable of making her life a misery win her. I don't fathom your logic. I doubt it exists in this matter. Besides, I am sick unto death of hearing about your reputation. You act like you're the only one who ever had one."

"Duncan, I am not convinced I'd make a good husband."

"I've never known a man who thought he was

unworthy for marriage. It has been my experience we're inclined to think we're rather superior and would make marvelous husbands. You are a queer fish. Why, do you expect to run around on her?"

"Good God, no! I would love her forever."

"Then offer for her. It's a good thing we don't have such timid soldiers. We'd be doomed to eventually hail Bonny as our emperor."

"You certainly put things in plain language. I've been given the advice to offer for her twice today. Perhaps I should consider it," Ward said. He placed his brandy glass on the table and rose to take his leave.

Duncan escorted him to the foyer. "Buck up, old man," he said, slapping Ward on the back. "You'll manage the whole affair. I have no doubts."

Leighton looked into the usually merry eyes of his friend and saw concern. "I'll consider it," he said.

Lord Leighton wandered aimlessly along the streets, deep in thought, and found himself walking along Bond Street pausing to shop-gaze. The Bond Street fashionables were promenading along the narrow street, and it reminded him of the well-known story told about the Prince of Wales. It is told that Charles Fox wagered the Prince on how many cats would be seen along the street, then promptly chose the sunny side. Winning the bet by a thirteen to none, Prinny ruefully paid the wager.

The anecdote lightened Ward's mood as he sauntered along, not minding the people passing by. He looked up to see Mary Beth Stewart and Angel Harlan admiring a bonnet in a shop window. It was as if his thoughts had caused Lady Harlan to appear. *Miss*

"Good morning, ladies."

Two heads snapped around. A look of dismay

appeared on Lady Stewart's face, and Ward nodded
to her. A fleeting expression of joy leapt into Lady
Harlan's eyes and just as quickly disappeared.

"Good morning, Lord Leighton," they said in
unison.

Ward shifted and glanced at the outrageous
bonnet they had been admiring. "Which of you two
ladies will chose that notable creation?"

"Neither, I think," Lady Harlan replied with
equal humor.

"May I escort you along the street?" Ward asked
with a racing heart. Never, never had he felt so like
a schoolboy, not even when he *was* a schoolboy.
That fanciful idea danced in his eyes with merry,
beguiling lights, not lost on the ladies.

"We would be delighted," Angel quickly
answered.

A small shadow crossed Mary Beth's eyes. The
man was dangerous, too fascinating by half, she
thought. A quick look at Angel sent her heart
tumbling to her weak knees. The most adorable,
silly expression had manifested itself on the angelic
face of her niece. The child gazed at the young man
as if he were a chivalrous knight with his foot
resting on a slain dragon. We are in trouble, Mary
Beth thought, and squared her shoulders to do
battle. She would rout this rake in an instant. She
opened her mouth to speak and closed it at the
sound of laughter from Angel.

The opportune moment passed and she found
herself trailing along the narrow sidewalk with the
couple. Shoppers crowded the walk and Mary Beth
was forced to step aside and then scamper to catch
up. Her two companions were totally unaware of
her existence, engaged as they were in a conversation that apparently was exceedingly amusing.
Mary Beth caught snatches of it and it didn't seem

that amusing—rather inane, actually. She watched them and realized it was not the small talk that was so exciting, but each other. Lord in heaven, she prayed, help us. Our Angel is falling . . . in love.

"Mary Beth, isn't that vastly amusing?" Angel said in obvious delight.

"Yes, dear, vastly." She turned to quell Lord Leighton's pretensions and met his eyes. She saw pleasure and pain. He seemed to say, Give me a chance. It was so heartfelt a look, Mary Beth dropped her eyes.

Lord have mercy on us, she sighed. Glancing up at him once more, she nodded. His eyes lit instantly, as if the sun came from behind a cloud. His captivating charm encompassed them all. Mary Beth realized she could do nothing else, no more than she could stay the ocean's tides.

13

Dear Libby.

Do forgive me. I have not written for ages. You can't imagine just how time-consuming and exhausting a Season is. It's actually harrowing. Take pity on me, my face is frozen in a permanent smile. Well, to the news at hand.

The Duke of Albrion has been paying me a tentative sort of courtship. No declaration has been forthcoming, but I think he is interested. I say "think" because one can't be too sure with the duke. When he smiles, it's as if he were bestowing a gift. Don't you think it odd to have the feeling someone is smiling at one on purpose? Not too surprising, for that is exactly what I do.

At any rate, he extended an invitation to visit his country seat. At first, I thought it was to meet his mother, for that is what he told me. We were out for a carriage ride at the time and encountered Lord Leighton in the company of the Duchess of de Aubrey. Upon the sight of the modern-day Helen of Troy, Lord Corners' eyes practically bugged out of his face. You would understand if you could see her. Believe me, I pale into insignificance in her presence. My milk-water complexion and coloring disappear next to the dark-haired beauty.

What bothers me most is that I did not mind the duke's drooling over the lady, yet I cared very much that she was in Lord Leighton's company. Does that mean what I think it does? Heaven help me. I wouldn't stand a chance against so gorgeous a lady. The idea is rather discouraging.

I do like Lord Corners, but I never seem to learn anything new about him. He remains the same: kind, courteous, and attentive. I see no devotion in his eyes. A speculative look, once in a while, that I cannot fathom or explain.

Lord Leighton, on the other hand, is known to be a ladies' man, but I never feel threatened with him, just gooseflesh. Oh, Libby, I fear the worse.

Mary Beth and I met Lord Leighton while shopping on Bond Street. I could see instant misgiving in Mary Beth's eyes. She watches me like a hawk. I have used all my thespian talents, mounted my wide-eyed expression of innocence and casual, disinterested pose concerning Leighton. I think I have been successful. I show proper, modest interest in Corners. It would never do for Mary Beth to know I think of Lord Leighton far too often. I was proud of my acting abilities and wouldn't you know Lord Leighton said, as we parted, "I look forward to seeing you at Lord Corners' party."

I could have died on the spot, for I had not mentioned that fact to Mary Beth. I thought for a moment she was about to have a fatal attack. All the way home, I heard a lecture about my staying clear of the dangerous man. Great heavens, Libby, how dangerous can a man be if you never get to be together?

Really, I think elders make far too much of it. Don't you? I shall write after I get back from the

weekend. Perhaps Lord Corners will propose. I
suppose I'll have to accept, but it would be much
more to my liking if it were Lord Leighton. I sigh
with regret that I am still a silly green girl instead
of an elegant lady, as is the Duchess of de Aubrey.
Libby, you will learn that mere airs do not make
one what one pretends to be. How does one become
glamorous?

Burn this letter. I shall write to tell you all.

Love,
Angel

Angel was correct. Mary Beth viewed the chance
encounter with more than misgivings. She was
terrified. Shaking her head in denial of her own
foolish acceptance of Angel's behavior at face value,
she knew full well her niece could make one believe
anything she desired. She had been taken in by
Angel's smiles for Lord Corners, the frequent conversation about the man, and her apparent pleasure
in his company. It was all a ruse. The chit's thoughts
were of Lord Leighton. Mary Beth remembered
coming upon her niece suddenly and seeing a
faraway look disappear in the blink of an eyelash.

Well, now I have the situation well in hand, Mary
Beth thought as she directed the packing for the
weekend. Understanding the truth, Mary Beth felt
a pang of compassion. Above all else, she wanted
Angel happy, for she deserved it. She had proven
herself a trooper and was the dearest young lady.
Angel could bedevil one to distraction, but there
wasn't an unkind bone in her body. Mary Beth
sighed. She shut her eyes against tears, understanding so well disappointment. Wiping away a
tear, Mary Beth decided to observe Angel this
weekend and make a decision. There is no chance
I'll permit Angel to wed where her heart is not,

Mary Beth vowed. She left the room to speak to her
father.

Angel busily directed the maids in her own
packing, unaware she had an ally to her future
happiness. An underlying excitement could not be
disguised by Angel despite her best acting abilities.
Her outstanding eyes shone with a sparkling
anticipation.

This state of affairs was not lost on Mary Beth
when she entered Angel's bedchamber. Dresses,
bonnets, and dozens of slippers were scattered over
the bed and chairs.

Mary Beth laughed. "You obviously need help."

"I cannot decide which gowns to take or which
bonnets. Do help me choose. I must be at my best."

"Really?"

Angel glanced up. "Well, I think the duke may
propose and we must consider the Duchess of de
Aubrey."

"We must? How so?"

"Mary Beth, I've never known you to be obtuse.
The duchess is the most beautiful woman I've ever
seen, and she accompanies Lord Leighton to
Marlefort. One minute the duke was discussing my
meeting his mother with veiled hints of offering for
me, the next he clapped his eyes on the fair duchess
at Leighton's side and fell over himself in his haste
to invite them. So suddenly, 'Meet Mother' becomes
a weekend house party. So you see, I must be at my
very best."

"Angel, why didn't you tell me all this before?"
Mary Beth said, looking askance at the intrigued
maids. She frowned. "We will choose the gowns and
you may return to pack them," she said, sending the
interested maids off. "Angel, watch what you say

before those silly girls. You can be sure all you have said will be repeated."

"I suppose so. I cannot figure men out. The gleam emanating from the duke's eyes was one I never evoked."

"Hmm, this places several possible connotations on the party. It will bode well if we are very observant," Mary Beth warned with a frown.

"Well, Leighton is the notorious rake and it's Albrion who practically pants over the beautiful duchess. I felt *de trop*, to be sure. I vouch the invitation he issued Leighton was grudgingly given."

"I can understand that. The priggish duke pitted against the compelling Lord Leighton is not a fair contest, though I doubt Corners has the humility to see that."

"Mary Beth! You shock me!"

"By stating the obvious?"

"Well, I don't want a husband that makes calf eyes at every pretty woman. In fact, I won't have one," Angel declared, placing her hands on her hips.

"You cannot fault a man for looking. It's their nature."

"Would he invite her if he just wanted to look?"

"Hmm, perhaps this is an advantage. We will judge the duke's behavior. Yes, let us pack your most flattering dresses. You will not be over-shadowed by the beautiful Duchess of de Aubrey!"

Angel laughed. "Mary Beth, you amaze me."

"Do I? Well, I suspect it is time you learned just what I think, so you spend less time convincing me what I should believe by your manipulating acting."

Angel gasped. "Mary Beth, you are acting very strange. I can't make you out."

"Well, then, just watch me. You'll soon learn what I really think."

Angel stood with a gaping mouth as the door flew open and Lord Stewart marched into the room.

"I've decided to accompany you to Marlefort. I think it singularly lacking on Lord Corners' part in neglecting to include me. I won't have my girl off in some wilderness setting without my careful eye on the proceedings," he said in a booming voice.

"Wilderness? It's the finest house in England."

"Makes no difference. You're my duty and I'll see that I tend to it."

"What would happen? I'm not about to make a cake of myself. Haven't I proved that? Or almost proved that?" Angel said in dismay.

"But of course. That is exactly why I join you both."

"What does that mean, Grandfather?"

"You silly goose, it means I'll be there to watch the proceedings and see that nothing amiss befalls you."

"Nothing amiss?"

Lord Stewart put out his chin in the expression that meant there would be no moving from his position. Angel had seen it often.

"Yes, Grandfather. I suspect we shall all be falling over one another with the growing population of a quiet weekend party," Angel said, and laughed at the comedy unfolding.

The butler softly cleared his throat at the open doorway. "Lord Hatton has come to call. He wishes to see Lady Angel, my lord."

Lord Stewart laughed. "I thought it would be a simple task to get you shackled. I should have known better." He left the room laughing all the way down the hall.

Angel looked at Mary Beth. "I look a sight. Tell him I'll join you both in a moment," she said. "I'll straighten my hair and slip on a more fetching dress."

"There's safety in numbers, I suppose," Mary Beth said, and chuckled as she left the room.

Angel joined Lord Hatton and Mary Beth within fifteen minutes. She looked as fresh as a spring daisy.

"Good morning, Lord Hatton," Angel said with a dazzling smile.

Mary Beth rolled her eyes.

"I have been in Bath to see my father and have just returned. I am delighted to find you home," he said, unable to hide the nervous tremor in his voice.

Amused, Mary Beth noted the bouquet he handed Angel was of more modest proportions than the first he had offered her.

"They are beautiful, thank you. Please be seated," Angel said.

He promptly did so and shifted uncomfortably in his chair. Mary Beth felt as though her presence was not desired, and nodded for him to speak out. She was not about to leave and have that silly boy pop the question. Angel was so impulsive, one could not be too careful.

"Would you honor me by attending a rout tomorrow at Lady Covington's?" he asked.

"Oh, I am sorry. I must decline. We are traveling to Marlefort for the weekend."

Lord Hatton paled and glanced nervously toward Mary Beth.

"I will see to some refreshments and will return in a moment," she said, rising swiftly and leaving the young couple alone.

"Is this an, er, official visit? I mean, is an announcement about to be made?" he asked.

"I do not think so, Lord Hatton. I am not sure I

wish to take a husband yet. I've just begun to enjoy the Season," she lied.

"I thought you didn't like the social whirl. I have heard you say so many times."

"I did? Well, I'm not sure."

"I understand about getting shackled too soon. Rather worrisome, don't you agree? I've told my father the very thing."

"Indeed? Then we are in agreement."

"May I call upon you when you return? My father would be most gratified. I mean, so would I, of course."

"Of course, Lord Hatton. You are always welcome. I do enjoy seeing you."

"You do? Well, now, that's more than I could hope for."

"How so? You are good company. I should think most people would benefit from your company," Angel said with the kindest smile.

"You do? Well, I am flattered to hear you say so." The young gentleman seemed to sit a little taller and take on a more confident air.

Angel's heart went out to him in sympathy. She knew he was bullied by his father, and a little confidence was all he needed.

"Yes," she said, "I think of you as a true friend."

"Friend, yes . . . friend. That is exactly it. We're friends," he said with a visible sigh of relief. He had managed to keep the door open for his calls without declaring and, thereby, keeping his father off his neck. He beamed. "Well, I must get on. Do have a pleasant weekend. I shall see you upon your return," he said, rising to take his leave.

Mary Beth entered the room. "Oh, you're leaving?"

"Have a thousand things to attend to," he replied, offering an elegant leg. He made a quick exit.

"He certainly scampered off," Mary Beth said. "What ever did you say to him?"

"He was grateful he did not have to offer for me. He's scared silly. I suspect his father is after my dowry. Ah, well, one's charm cannot win all," Angel said, laughing until the tears rolled down her cheeks.

Mary Beth smiled. "Angel, you would try the patience of a saint. Why can't you just find a nice young man and settle, once and for all? I need some peace. This is devilishly trying."

"Ah, but not boring, you must admit."

"Reluctantly, to be sure."

14

Marlefort, which lay east of Henley-on-Thames among slightly rolling terrain, was famous throughout England. Every guidebook described the unique architectural beauty of this magnificent structure, which was built in the mid-seventeenth century.

The west facade incorporated bold classical themes. It was a vibrant composition set into motion by a rusticated double staircase rising to a high terrace. The ground floor was boldly rusticated and supported huge, fluted Ionian pilasters, which rose to support a carved frieze. The colossal pediment was richly carved with classical figures engaged in the Trojan War. The frieze supported a balustraded parapet. Roman gods graced the parapet in direct line to the pilasters, giving unity and a feeling of ascending design of dramatic impetus. Tall windows enhanced the upward thrust with large keystones and carved garlands.

The use of Roman and Greek motifs had not seemed incongruous to the builders, and added a fanciful touch to the knowledgeable observer. The overall impact was one of exuberance and proved to be a forerunner of future Baroque design. It may have influenced Vanbrugh almost a half-century later.

The carriage of the Marquess of Farnham sped over the rising road nearing Marlefort. As it reached the top of the knoll, the mansion came into view and the passengers exclaimed in unison at the beautiful structure, magnificent even from a distance.

Marlefort's monumental size would subdue the most-seasoned traveler, and Angel was no exception. She stared in awe as the carriage halted in front of the entrance. The Duke of Albrion honored his guests by descending the steps to personally greet them. This distinction was not lost on Lord Stewart.

Corners wore a leather coat, breeches, and high boots. His hair and eyes were enhanced by the rich brown of his excellent coat. His broad shoulders and athletic body moved with ease as he approached the carriage.

"Welcome to Marlefort," the duke said, offering a bow and a broad smile that was no less than lighthearted. A liveried servant let down the steps and the duke stepped in to assist the ladies.

"Your grace, Marlefort is more beautiful than any description could possibly convey," Angel said, her face raised to view the imposing edifice.

The duke smiled with pride, for he loved this house, its history, and its beauty. "Come, your journey has been tiring. Your servants arrived this morning and all is in order for your comfort. You may wish to freshen yourselves and then, perhaps, some refreshments. I am elated you are here at last." His gaze lingered on her face.

Angel hated herself when she blushed, but this gratified the duke, for he believed his future wife should be of delicate, modest demeanor.

Corners took Angel's arm, leaving the others to

follow. "When you are rested, or perhaps tomorrow, I shall be honored to show you the interiors. We are fortunate our ancestors were men of taste to provide such a legacy for all future dukes of Albrion."

"You have made no change?" Angel asked.

"Only in the gardens, and they are at their showy best, just to please you. I ordered it so, you see," he said with a twinkle of humor.

"I am sure that is so, your grace."

He nodded approval and ushered his guests into the vast house. The hall reflected the energetic style of the facade, with carved woods and opulent plaster ceilings.

Farnsworth, the majordomo, and Mrs. Brantley, the housekeeper, met the arrivals at the foot of the stairs. Mary Beth and Angel followed Mrs. Brantley up the curved stairs and along paneled corridors to their respective rooms. Coolly indicating their rooms, Mrs. Brantley told them to ring for anything they might need. It was evident the house was run with clockwork precision.

Angel was relieved to find Jeanne placing the last of her gowns in a wardrobe. Her familiar face eased the tension of this overwhelming house and circumstance.

"You're a welcome sight, Jeanne," Angel exclaimed as she removed her hat. Her glance skimmed the sumptuous bedchamber, and she sighed.

Jeanne curtsied. "It's a veritable palace. One could get lost in these halls."

Angel nodded. "I fear even in this room."

The walls were paneled wainscot with rose brocade above. The huge bed was dressed in matching fabric and miles of gold silk fringe. High windows let in considerable light, which relieved the room from being oppressive. Fine furniture and *objets d' art* expressed the artistic taste of the duke. The room offered the comfortable feeling of time-honored elegance that would last forever.

"I have ordered water for a bath and some tea. I knew you would have need of both," Jeanne said, looking speculatively toward her mistress.

Angel nodded, wondering at her lack of enthusiasm. Perhaps it was all just too overwhelming. Surely one could get used to such a home in time, she supposed.

Jeanne opened the door to a soft knock and liveried footmen filed in carrying a large metal tub. Servants followed and poured hot water into the vessel, to which Jeanne added sweet oils from alabaster jars provided for their use. When the servants departed, Jeanne arranged the screens around the tub.

Angel disrobed and slipped into the warm, comforting water. Closing her eyes, she gave herself up to the warmth of the water, which soothed every tired muscle. Her tenseness faded and she relaxed for the first time since the journey began.

Jeanne wrapped her mistress in a large monogrammed towel to dry as Angel stepped from the tub. Tying a silk robe around her slender waist, Angel sipped tea while Jeanne brushed her pale hair.

"Now, rest, Lady Angel, I shall call you in time to dress for dinner."

Angel was happy to obey and drifted off to sleep in a matter of minutes.

Jeanne stepped back and admired Lady Angel's appearance. She wore a slim dress of the finest muslin trimmed with delicate *point de Venise*. A necklace of pearls looped up with small sapphires matched her earrings and brought out the color of her eyes. She carried a finely woven blue cashmere shawl.

"You look lovely, Lady Angel. No one will be able to take their eyes off you," Jeanne boasted.

"You are decidedly partial," Angel answered.

Mary Beth entered looking neat and subdued. She wore a dove gray silk gown also trimmed in lace. The no-nonsense style of her dress matched the expression on her face.

"Angel, you'll take the duke's breath away. No wonder he is enamored," Mary Beth said with forced enthusiasm.

Angel returned a weak smile.

"Where is my actress? Let us see the brilliant toast of the Season reappear," Mary Beth challenged.

Angel laughed and turned on an enchanting smile. "Perfect!"

"Let's hope I can maintain it," Angel said just as a footman arrived to escort them through the confusing corridors and down to the drawing room.

Both ladies caught their breath as they entered the magnificent room. Mortlake tapestries from Raphael's famous cartoon of the *Acts of the Apostles*, which graced the Vatican, hung from the walls. Each tapestry was framed by egg-and-dart carvings. The ceiling had been painted by Verrio and the wood carvings had been created by Watson. Watson never attained the three-dimensional naturalism of Gringling Gibbons, but he had managed to create a totality of lighthearted design. The room was gorgeous.

The Duke of Albrion, looking handsome as ever, crossed the floor and took Angel's hand. "Come and allow me to introduce you to my mother."

Angel's eyes rested on a seated lady of great nobility. Tall and ramrod-straight, she sat dressed in black with diamonds sparkling at her throat and on all fingers. Her snow-white hair was piled on her head and encircled with a diamond tiara.

Lady Corners scrutinized the tiny young woman as she approached on her son's arm. She seemed a bit too fragile. None could fault her looks, for she was lovely. The duchess glanced to her son and was surprised at his matter-of-fact expression. She looked again to Lady Harlan and wondered if this pale, slender lady could hold her son's robust interest. She dismissed the thought immediately, as though it had no significance. The child would simply have to adjust to what most women had to accept. It made no difference, the girl was more than lucky to have secured her son's interest.

Angel dropped a fine curtsy, and her eyes met those of the duchess as she rose. They showed no emotion as the grand lady nodded.

"We are delighted to have you visit Marlefort, Lady Harlan. We hope your stay is agreeable and that we come to know you better."

My heavens, thought Angel, she uses the royal we. There's the indication of her self-importance. It was natural that Angel's spirits fell considerably, causing her to send the duke a faltering look. He smiled encouragement.

"I am honored to be here," Angel replied.

The duke next introduced Mary Beth Stewart and Lord Stewart, and the duchess greeted them with the same regal politeness. For once, Lord Stewart hid his dynamic nature and moved off with a decided scowl upon his face. For the first time, he was in doubt of his Angel's happiness. He realized it was one thing to make a brilliant marriage and quite another to perish in one. His Angel deserved more than a disapproving, self-important aristocrat for a mother-in-law. These Corners were no better than the Stewarts, and just because his daughter made a mistake, it was not to be held against a fair and lovely granddaughter. He would not allow that. He bristled.

Well, I shall monitor this situation and, believe me, he thought, no one will cause my Angel a moment of sorrow. He would take note of all the undercurrents this weekend. He had won his success by understanding the nature and weaknesses of men. Now he would use that gift to secure Angel's happiness.

The dowager duchess continued to watch Angel as the duke led her to meet the other guests. Aware of this scrutiny, Angel had to call on all her discipline to resist the urge to run, screaming, from the room. Her fixed smile twitched a little as her eyes caught Lord Leighton standing next to the Duchess of de Aubrey.

The duchess wore lavender with a magnificent amethyst necklace. Her warm eyes glowed and she smiled at Angel. "I am pleased to meet you again, Lady Harlan. I can see why you have captured the heart of every London beau," she said with gentle kindness.

Surprised, Angel glanced to Lord Leighton.

He bowed. "Good evening, Lady Harlan."

Angel dropped a curtsy and returned the greeting, secretly enjoying the tingle that ran through her body.

The duke began an extended conversation. He was plainly interested in every utterance the duchess made, for he watched her mouth with undivided interest.

Angel was aware of his fascination for the lady, and when his gaze traveled to her well-rounded bosom, Angel smiled. I wonder if he thinks she speaks with that well-displayed part of her body. The thought brought a devilish smile to Angel's heretofore passive expression.

Lord Leighton's amusement brought a twinkle to his eyes, which Angel recognized immediately. Drat the man, Angel thought. It's as if Leighton reads my mind. She repressed the overwhelming desire to stick her tongue out at him. He seemed so confident, standing there like a peacock, while Lord Corners makes a veritable fool of himself. She snapped open her fan and fanned her hot cheeks.

The duchess was not amused by the duke's ogling eyes and simultaneously snapped open her fan to cover the fascinating view from his gaze. Angel almost giggled when she recognized the duchess's action and their eyes met in understanding.

This bit of encouragement from the duchess made Angel unable to resist the urge, and she stepped firmly on Lord Corner's foot. So tiny a foot, encased in satin, caused no more than the startled look upon the duke's face.

"I am so sorry, your grace. You should have looked where you moved," Angel said, her large blue eyes wide with pure innocence.

"I didn't move."

"Ah, but I beg to differ with you. Perhaps you were too engrossed in the conversation to notice," she sweetly replied.

Lord Corners was horrified. How dare she correct him?

"Indeed, your grace, I thought for a minute you had lost your balance," Madeleine de Aubrey purred. "Are you well?"

The duke was suddenly without speech. To his great relief dinner was announced. He smiled and moved to offer his mother his arm.

15

The family dining room was not as grand or elaborate as the state room and, therefore, offered warmth and intimacy. It was proportionately as beautiful as the salon, with exquisite carvings and paintings. Candles glowed and flickered, giving an appealing beauty to the room, as did the sparkling crystal and fragrant flowers. This enchanting setting was pleasing and conveyed an amiable atmosphere.

It was a cordial duke who sat himself at the head of the table. Any annoyance he held was not in evidence. He became the caring, perfect host, interested in the comfort of all his guests. The Duchess of de Aubrey, who sat to his right, as befitted her rank, skeptically raised a delicate eyebrow. Lord Leighton, placed to her right, watched the duke's artful charm with hidden disdain. The dowager Duchess of Albrion, who graced the foot of the table, beamed with maternal pride that knew no bounds.

Angel, sitting to her right as a mark of distinction, fell under the spell of the duke's obvious charm. Her vexation toward her host faded as she watched him. He *was* handsome and genial. Perhaps, she thought, I was rude. He obviously meant no more than undesigning interest in Madeleine de Aubrey. She had misjudged him, and she dropped her eyes in shame. No one could be so genuinely kind and harbor evil thoughts for guests in his own home. She regretted her hasty and unkind opinions of him.

Lord Stewart relented, for perhaps his grand-daughter was going to be offered a happy union. Mary Beth merely watched the duke, who seemed to be as changeable as English weather. She would make her judgment on more than manners.

The size of the party allowed a more general conversation, rather than most parties, which confined one to the persons sitting on either side. Lord Corners made every effort to bring each guest into the discourse and graciously led it with unfeigned *savoir-faire*.

A pause in the conversation allowed Lady Corners to turn to Angel. "How have you enjoyed the Season thus far? I hear from my friends you have become the standard which all mothers charge their daughters to emulate. Your modesty and grace have captured many young beaux, I am told."

Angel almost choked on her sip of wine. She was caught off-guard, and a blush materialized, her hand trembling as she set her glass down. Eyes wide with incredulity, Angel stared at Lady Corners. How does one answer so excessive a compliment? she wondered.

"I hardly merit such praise," Angel finally uttered.

"Nonsense, child, I would not have said it if I had not heard the very thing."

Angel glanced to Lord Leighton, who sat directly across from her, and saw a bland expression of polite veneer. Her eyes traveled to Lord Corners, who sat displaying an annoying, proprietary smile.

"Mother, you embarrass our modest Lady Harlan with your high praise, though I must concur," he said with a soft laugh. "Let us toast our blushing friend for her modesty," Corners said, raising his glass to her.

I am going to die right here and right now, Angel thought. She looked directly into Lord Corner's eyes and wondered if she glimpsed spite. Ever so fleeting, to be sure, but she was positive it had been there.

Everyone joined the toast, and Angel's hackles rose. To single one out in such a manner was rude. She caught Madeleine de Aubrey's eyes and saw the compassion in them. A relief filled Angel's heart and she returned the smile. Why, the beautiful duchess is in sympathy with me.

Suddenly, Angel felt immersed in a charade, with everyone inventing a role to play, herself included. This is bizarre, she thought, and defiantly lifted her chin.

She turned to Leighton and he smiled with a little nod of support. He too understood! A radiant smile lit her face, illuminating her beauty to nothing short of breathtaking.

Lady Corners let out a gasp of air. Angel turned to her and said, "Your kindness is overwhelming. I shall remember it always." The silky tones did not disguise the hint of sarcasm.

Leighton chuckled. Angel dared not look at him or she would succumb to laughter. She bit her tongue to stay the impulse, remembering his very effective way of stopping giggles.

The dowager perceived something in Angel she had not expected, and looked to her son. Mayhap, this seemingly mild young lady was more than he might wish to handle. There was far more to her than the fragile countenance.

Lord Corners altogether missed the subtle byplay. He sat in the self-satisfied world of his perfection.

The long protracted meal ended, but not before the duke offered his opinions on the duties of the elite to help the poor. He glanced around the table for approval and interpreted each gaze as just that.

"In honor of our charming ladies, let us forgo our port and join them directly," the duke said, rising from the table. He was not about to spend time with the insufferable Leighton and boorish Stewart.

"While the light still holds, allow me to take you about the rose garden," Corners said, taking Angel's arm.

She stole a furtive peek at Leighton, but he was speaking with the other guests and paying no attention to her. Admonishing herself to firmly put Leighton from her mind, she vowed not to care whether the marquess looked at her or not. Grow up, she told herself, just because he understands doesn't mean he cares. She turned to the duke and smiled.

Dusk was falling and the early-evening air was fresh and cool. Angel pulled her shawl around her shoulders and crossed the terrace, her hand resting on the duke's arm. The rose garden was glorious and the fragrance heavenly. They walked together for a while in silence.

"You once said you love the country. Does Marlefort please you?"

"Yes, your grace, it is lovely. Magnificent would be more to the point. Hardly subjected to any country inconvenience," she said, casting a coy glance.

"No, but town pleasures are absent," he replied.

"No loss, to my thinking."

"Perhaps, for a time, but I am sure you would soon desire the company of London society."

She turned to him. "In all truthfulness, I would not. I have found nothing I would miss."

A flicker crossed his fine dark eyes. "You would be content to remain here?"

"Yes, very content in the country, your grace." She very carefully avoided confirming the word "here."

"Please call me William. For the sake of argument, would you remain while your husband tended to his business in town?"

"Not if he wished me to come, but if he had business to attend and I would be of no help, I would remain in the country. Of course, if I married someone who only liked London, then I would have to learn to prefer it also."

"Ah, but that would not be equable. I suppose most marriages flourish better with some absence. Do you agree?"

"I can hardly say, since I have not been married."

He laughed. "You're correct, of course. It would be necessary to make an arrangement that suited both parties," he said, and gave her hand a little squeeze.

They walked on without speaking. Suddenly the duke stopped. He reached up and placed his hand along her cheek. "You are an enchanting lady. I may be old-fashioned, but I am going to speak to your grandfather. I shall come to you after I have his approval. You would make me an admirable wife. No, don't answer yet. First, let me speak to your grandfather. It will also give you time to consider what I have said. I would not for the world rush you into a decision."

"I am taken by surprise."

"Precisely, and it is understandable. I will come to you when you have thought it over. Please do not mention this to anyone. I will ask your grandfather and speak to my mother first." The duke felt uneasy that the girl before him had not leapt at the prospect with rapture. He was, after all, the catch. Still, he admired her restraint and judged it as such.

"Does your mother approve of me? You could marry wherever you desired, I'm sure."

He laughed. "Angel, you flatter me and do not give enough credit to your worthiness. You are beautiful and would grow into the finest of duchesses. It is a demanding position. I do not take it lightly. My duty is to my family and the future generations. I hold that responsibility to be a trust. I could never treat my charge with the indifference of Leighton."

"Your diligence to your position is to be admired," she said dryly.

"Thank you, my dear. I knew you would view it as such. That is exactly why I am pleased with you."

"If you scorn Leighton's conduct, why did you invite him this weekend?"

Lord Corners flinched. He pursed his lips. "I have said too much. It is not my practice to gossip. I beg your pardon, but I feel sorry for the Duchess of de Aubrey. Perhaps by my example, Lord Leighton will take note and settle himself."

"With the beautiful duchess?" Angel asked with a tremble in her voice.

"I should think he will need a more worldly lady, and she would suit that purpose."

Angel nodded. "I suppose, and she *is* lovely."

A disturbing image of Leighton with the duchess filled Corners' mind, but he skillfully hid his reaction with a shrug. "If one likes that sort of lady,

I should say you are correct. My choice is definitely of a higher plane."

Righteousness was clearly his aegis, indicated by his self-assured manner and insipid pronouncements. He smiled. His eyes were gentle and his manner solicitous when he took her arm to return to the salon.

My heavens, Angel thought, I've surpassed all that grandfather could wish. I am worthy of perpetuating the noble line of the Albrions. The honor should apparently leave me overwhelmed with gratitude. She masked her thought with an innocuous expression. Affection, love, or attachment had never entered the conversation. She shook her head in dismay, and the flaxen curls bobbed.

"Angel, this is not all I wish to say. First let me speak to your grandfather, then we'll talk."

"Yes, your grace," she replied listlessly.

Albrion lifted her hand to his lips. He turned it over and kissed the inside and raised his warm brown eyes to hers.

Passively watching until he dropped her hand, she quickened her steps toward the manor. She would have run if it had been seemly.

16

Angel sat on the edge of her bed, feet dangling over and her hands folded in her lap. She reviewed the evening with mixed emotions. It had been pleasant in some ways. Lord Corners was the perfect host, none could deny that.

Angel frowned at the thought of his mother. She had been peered at, judged, and examined like some upstart by the stiff-rumped old dowager, who fairly doted on her admittedly handsome son. *I seriously doubt anyone could come up to snuff as a daughter-in-law, least of all me.*

What can I say for him? I like him well enough, but he is difficult to know. He does all the right things, as if he is trying to convince everyone of how nice he is. That's it. That's exactly what he is doing. Why?

She shrugged. The answer remained with the other mysteries of life such as: why does it always rain during picnics or why does one's hair behave only when there's no place to go? Unable to bear another noble pronouncement by William, she had escaped as soon as was possible, feigning fatigue.

She liked him well enough. What was there not

to like? Unless it was self-praising remarks at every opportunity and the pronouncements of his noble behavior, all the while casting disdainful looks to the scandalous Lord Leighton. Why had Corners invited someone he considered unworthy? In hopes of converting him or in hopes of getting the Duchess of de Aubrey in his clutches? No, that simply was not so, for Corners was obviously a principled man.

Angel had already gone over these thoughts a dozen times, and to no avail. In exasperation, she slid off the bed. Sleep was as elusive as these answers to her questions. Slipping on a robe, she began to pace the floor like a Newgate prisoner. She stopped dead in her tracks. Leighton! Now there was a strange one. His charismatic personality couldn't be dimmed by Albrion's aspersions, however veiled. He had taken the barbs with a wry smile. Angel chuckled. Leighton had actually been amused by the whole scenario.

She could not shake the feeling that she was in harmony with him. It seemed as though he knew what she was thinking all through the evening. While it was comforting, it was also unnerving.

With an impatient gesture, she pushed back her hair, which hung in a cascade about her shoulders. Here I am, about to accept the duke's offer, and then where will I be? Another mealymouthed wife nodding her head like a court jester. Great heavens, would she ever forget the horrified look that popped on Lord Corners' face when she stepped on his toes? What delicious fun! Leighton had been amused.

Anyhow, Leighton hadn't spent the evening trying to see down Madeleine de Aubrey's bodice. Angel's heart gave a lurch. Maybe he didn't have to . . . maybe he had that privilege privately. Oh, no, dear God, don't let that be so!

The tedium of being married to a man holier than

the pope stretched before her. I'll remain single. I'll buy little brown and gray dresses, like Mary Beth, and do as I please. That's exactly what I'll do.

Grandfather seemed so pleased, and I can't disappoint him. If only the duke were not so pious and Leighton not so naughty and knowing . . . Maybe she could talk Leighton into reforming, but with a beauty like Madeleine, that hope faded instantly.

Angel continued pacing with the same thoughts repeating themselves *ad nauseam*. The room was dark, with only the palest moonlight shimmering through the windows.

A creak caught Angel's attention. She stood still to listen. Another creak was followed by a series of them. It was the sound of someone treading stealthily near her room. How odd! She looked to the wall from where the sound came. A pale sliver of light gleamed through a crack that ran down the paneled wall. She walked softly to stand next to the wall and leaned her ear close to it. The light became slightly stronger, as did the footsteps. They passed directly on the other side of the wall, then began to fade away.

The lure of this curious phenomenon was more than this young lady could resist. She spun around quickly and ran to her bedside table to light a taper. Returning to the wall, she raised the flickering candle and ran her hand along the carved paneling. There was something on the other side of the wall. She could feel cool air issuing from the crack, and the flame on the candle flickered when she passed it back and forth over the tiny gap. Searching along the carvings, her fingers touched a carved Tudor rose that shifted under her touch. She carefully turned the carved rose, and her eyes grew wide as the panel creaked open.

With a pounding heart she paused. Should she

open the small door and peek out? She did. Her caution had lasted no more than a second. Tentatively, she peered out into blackness. The passing light had disappeared with the soft footsteps. Who had gone by, and to what purpose? She knew such passages were sometimes used by smugglers, but Marlefort was far from the sea, so that wasn't likely. She hesitated a moment, took a breath, and stepped forward into the dark, narrow corridor. Her candle offered only a pale pool of light and her vision was limited to that small space.

The passage had probably been built with the original house. She took a tentative step forward. She wanted to find out who had crept by. She had to know! The possible answer horrified her.

Silently she moved along the dusty passageway; her small weight caused no creaking noise. The candle flickered dangerously, and the frightening thought of being stranded in the dark crossed her mind. Undaunted, she moved forward, counting the doors that lined the corridor so that she could find her own. A crack of light shone from under the third door and she paused to listen.

She remained still, but there was no sound. She decided to open the door a bit, to see what this mystery was all about. Angel began to turn the knob slowly. A door opened farther along the corridor, and she heard the echo of voices as the light suddenly streamed into the passageway.

Panic seized her. She must not be discovered. Unthinking, she pushed open the door and stepped inside, so as not to be found standing in the corridor in her nightdress and robe. Her heart pounded in her temples. Drat it, I've done it again! I've foolishly walked straight into a predicament.

The room was dim and apparently empty. Sighing with relief, she leaned one ear against the paneling and listened. Sure enough, the steps creaked along the other side of the wall again. Whoever it was began retracing his or her steps. She decided to open the panel and take a peek.

An arm pushed past her shoulder, and a hand held the panel door closed.

"It would not be wise to open that panel," a resonant masculine voice whispered in her ear.

She jumped with a start and a squeak. She whirled around and there stood a shoeless Lord Leighton, naked to the waist. She gasped.

Leighton put a finger to his lips to quiet her. She stared at his bare chest. Never had she considered what a half-naked man would look like, nor that it could be so pleasing a sight.

He watched her in amusement, his eyes glittering.

The candle cast a shading that emphasized his finely muscled torso. Fine, light hair covered his chest and tapered to his slim waist. Her heart thumped in her bosom, and the candle flickered in her trembling hand.

He smiled a wicked smile. "My dear, I am overwhelmed. I had not thought my charms were so irresistible," he said, taking the candle from her hand.

She hissed, "You know they're not."

"Then, why do I feel as Madeleine must have, with Corners ogling her?"

"I'm not ogling. I've never seen a man before . . . naked."

"My dear, I am not naked, but if your curiosity is such that—"

"Don't you dare," she interrupted. She stepped back into the wall.

"What in God's name are you doing here, if not to ogle?" There was obvious amusement at her expense.

"I heard someone go by and saw a sliver of light through a crack in the paneling. I naturally became curious, so I found the trick to open the panel."

"Naturally," he replied, but he caressed the word just as his eyes caressed her body. He reached out his hand and drew her hard against his strong, lean torso.

Angel's knees buckled from the overpowering feelings that erupted in her body.

He slowly bent his head and she watched with wide eyes as his lips covered hers. A warm tingling sensation filled her with delicious awareness. She closed her eyes and raised her arms around his neck. He trembled.

He could feel her soft rounded curves, and passion reared its inevitable head. It occurred to him that if he could feel her warm, soft body, then she could certainly feel his. Here he was, standing in knit breeches for all to see.

He drew away, his eyes gleaming in the dim light. He studied her lovely face, aglow with the emotions she little understood. His mind reeled.

Angel's curiosity was aroused and she started to glance down. Leighton's hands shot out and his fingers raised her chin. Damn, he stood embarrassed as a schoolboy!

"What are you here for?" he asked hoarsely as he drew back.

She felt the cool air come between them and almost stepped back into his arms. She checked that impulse. "I told you," she whispered, her chin still captured by his fingers.

"If you're found here, you'll have to marry me and not your precious duke." He spat the words.

She jumped. "I didn't mean to find you."

"What if you had entered the duke's room?

Would he be so anxious to make you his wife or perhaps just his mistress?"

"I didn't think. I mean, I never intended to go into anyone's room."

"So you followed a light in a hidden passage. Oh, Angel, what is to become of you?" he said. "You need a keeper. I swear, I never saw such a green, impulsive girl."

Tears filled her eyes. "At least I do something," she said in self-defense, somehow implying he did not.

"We've no time to discuss our respective faults. We've got to get you back without anyone knowing you were here."

"I can find my own way," she said, and lifted her chin in the most arrogant manner she could muster.

Leighton handed her the candle and opened the door to the passage. He made sure it was empty of midnight Romeos.

"Can you find your door?"

"Yes, the third one," she whispered back.

His eyes watched her and his lips twitched. "I would not tell anyone else, my dear, or you may have midnight visitors." He laughed softly, took her arm, and gently pushed her into the passage. It was the hardest thing he had ever done. He watched as she tiptoed along the corridor.

She turned and saw him still standing in the dim light from his room. The light shone off his tousled hair. Oh, my, she thought as she stepped back into her room.

Softly closing the door, she stood transfixed. She leaned against the hidden door and closed her eyes. She knew exactly why she had been so bold as to creep down a dusty, spooky, hidden passage in the dark of night. She had wanted to know if the footsteps belonged to Leighton and if he were seeking the duchess's bedchamber. That was the bald truth. Her heart tumbled over and over.

Happiness filled her, for it had not been Leighton. He was alone, in his own room. The duchess wasn't his lover. She had risked much to find out, but it had been worth it.

17

"Did Corners come to your room last evening?" Leighton asked in a confidential manner, his head bent near hers.

"But of course. You are not surprised, I'm sure. He was no trouble to discourage," Madeleine answered, her soft eyes glowing with amusement.

They stood in the dining room with the morning sunlight streaming in through the tall, leaded-pane windows. They looked like morning and midnight standing next to each other. He, with the sun gleaming golden lights on his hair, and she, in a black serge riding habit with her jet hair, stood as a handsome pair by anyone's standard.

"I was uneasy and about to come to your rescue when I heard his retreating steps in the hidden pasage not long after he had stealthily crept before. I knew you had routed him, for not even he is that expeditious," Leighton said with a villainous chuckle.

She softly laughed. "Would you have burst into

the room to save my virtue, had he not abandoned his pursuit so quickly? I swear, it was almost unflattering; however, I think he feared he might have a screaming banshee on his hands."

"My dear, I am always at your service," he said, and bowed in mock servility.

"Leighton, you're incorrigible. As you can see, I am beholden to ride with him this morning. I could do no less for the disappointed man," she said with her engaging, silvery laugh.

"Take heed, for there's no trusting that knave."

"Leighton, I've never known a lady to be ravished while seated sidesaddle on a horse, and there is not the man alive who could unseat me."

"You are confident of your equestrian talents."

"I had little else to do while married to de Aubrey. I am most proficient."

Leighton smiled and took her hand and raised it to his lips.

At the moment of this enchanting sight, Lord Corners entered the room with Lady Harlan trailing behind. Angel's steps faltered with dismay and a flutter skipped in her chest. Rankled, Corners hid his loathing of Leighton with amiable, good-morning greetings.

"Are you ready for our morning ride, Duchess?" Corners asked pleasantly.

Angel turned to Corners with an astonished expression that bordered on embarrassment. Obviously he was dressed for riding, but it was also obvious that he had previously arranged an outing with the duchess. Angel stood gaping, struggling all the while to suppress her chagrin. Her glance traveled to the duchess, who returned a gentle smile.

"I am anxious for the exercise. The duke has been so kind to humor me. Shall we go?" Madeleine asked as she moved away from Leighton. All eyes followed her as she gracefully took Corners' arm. "We'll be back soon," she promised.

Leighton, standing in the sunlight, watched her quietly but said nothing. He had crossed his arms and rested against the window frame. Angel could not read his thoughts; his face seemed void of expression.

"Well, a ride should be lovely. It is a very pretty day," she said rather feebly.

Dropping his arms, he pushed away from the wall and moved toward her. "Angel, take a turn about the garden with me. We can breakfast later. I want to speak with you."

Her first reaction was to agree in defiance of the duke. After all, she needn't sit around while Albrion rode off with a beauty. She couldn't really be jealous—or could she?

She nodded agreement to Leighton's suggestion. Her consent came from the sole desire to walk with him. Her pride was bruised, for she did not understand. Why would Corners go off with the duchess when he was practically to the point of proposing, unless that was not the case?

Ward crossed the room and came to stand before her. He offered his arm, "Come, let's enjoy the gardens. We'll ride later, if you wish."

She took his arm and looked into his eyes, twinkling with humor. Bemused, she smiled because she was suddenly happy.

*   *   *

They walked in the soft balmy air of the late-spring morning. Bees hummed busily among the roses. Delphiniums stood stately among the daisies and primroses. The air and the fragrances caressed them just as the warmth of the sun did. Nature smiled this morning, wearing her loveliest raiment. All creatures seemed to be in harmony, and so the fair couple walked among nature's beauty in a world of their own.

"Angel, I meant no insult last evening. You looked far too irresistible. The adventure of your imprudent actions made your beautiful eyes shine with an overwhelming power. You stood before me in your vulnerable beauty and I was lost. You are a bedeviling lady, and I am not resistant to your beguiling charm. Will you forgive me? I begged forgiveness once before and vowed never to overstep our friendship again. Still, I am a sinner and could not resist kissing you. Please understand I meant no offense. I apologize, yet it is hypocritical of me to say so, for I should like to do so again."

"Lord Leighton, it is my understanding that is not an unnatural state for you. Do not concern yourself with the matter. In all honesty, it was agreeable to me."

He did not reply as they continued to walk.

She peeked at him from the corner of her eyes and saw his jaw muscle tighten. She frowned. I am too outspoken, she thought.

"Do forgive me, I speak too boldly."

"No, Angel, it is natural to enjoy a kiss. You are uniquely honest, a virtue rarely found today. Take my advice and be careful to whom you would speak so frankly. It could easily be misun-

derstood, or worse, advantage taken. Please take
care."

Angel became outraged. "You gallantly apologize
for foisting yourself on me, then have the audacity
to warn me of such dangers. Doesn't that strike you
as the very duplicity that you are so wont to
espouse? Are you a moral tutor for the rest of the
world? If I want to kiss someone back, I shall do
so, and you have no right to warn, admonish, or
object."

"I'm thinking of your welfare," he said.

She stopped dead in her tracks. "Indeed, you
are? You kiss me, then apologize. What am I to
think? That's quite all right for Lord Leighton?
I need the practice? You're a fool, Lord Leighton, and I hope you end up with a shrew who
hounds you day and night." She turned on her
heels, lifted her skirts, and ran along the garden
path.

Damn Leighton, damn Corners. They could all go
to hell's fire. How could her mother have even cared
for any stupid man. They held no regard for anyone's feelings but their own. Women were mere con-
veniences. I'll never, never be in anyone's pocket.
She ran on breathlessly.

"If I marry, it will be to someone I care nothing
for. Affection only brings pain," she cried aloud to
herself as she neared the manor.

Ward stood helplessly still. What a clumsy fool
he was. How had his apology turned into such a
grievance for her? He had meant to smooth over his
misconduct. One simply did not kiss a lady of her
station without offering marriage. He had been
dreadfully wrong. She was never out of his
thoughts. He was a fool, a dolt, and because he was
so clumsy, he had offended her. Never had he felt

so alone, with such a bleak future stretching before him.

The Duke of Albrion emerged from his conference with Lord Stewart with a smug expression on his face. It had gone well. Angel's dowry was considerable, and while he was rich enough, it was gratifying to have more. She would be agreeable and pliable, the sort of wife he needed.

De Aubrey had given no promises, but he could tell she was taken with his charm. He could always tell when a lady was enamored. Madeleine de Aubrey was no different. Only Angel seemed remote and aloof. He would change that. Life was good, and all stretched before him with interesting opportunities.

He went in search of Angel to convey the happy news of her grandfather's consent, and finding her in the library reading surprised him. The horrifying thought that she might be a bluestocking occurred to him, for he really knew very little about her.

"My dear," he said, crossing the room with outstretched arms. "I have just spoken with your grandfather. He has consented to our marriage— that is, of course, if you are quite willing." He took her hands and raised her up.

He looked at her impassive, lovely face, and an eerie tremor passed through his body. She was beyond his reach, she remained untouched by his announcement. Annoyed, he bent his head to kiss her.

Angel stood enigmatically still and watched him come close. His lips were cool and his kiss chaste.

He looked into those dark-rimmed eyes. Her eyes were spectacular, yet they seemed as cold as ice. His kiss had left her untouched, and annoyance surged up. He pressed a more passionate kiss on her lips as if to will a passionate response.

"My lord, you are too anxious," she said, and stepped back.

"Excuse me, my dear. You are enchanting, my feelings for you overwhelm me," he said smoothly.

She took his measure and did not believe him. Leighton had been more indiscreet, yet she had believed he meant what he had said. That is why it hurt so. Leighton had kissed her but didn't want her. The duke didn't really care for her and yet wished to marry her. She would have to take the duke's offer. It was as good as she'd get. It had to be done, and she instinctively knew Albrion was not in love with her and would not seek her company often. She would merely bear his children and be left to her own devices. This suited her, and so she accepted the duke's honorable offer.

"You make me the happiest of men," he said, and kissed her hand. "We're certain to deal well together. You do me honor."

"A pretty speech, my lord. You are correct: we will deal well together. You will not find me a tiresome wife. I know that is what you would wish."

"Thank you, my dear. We will announce our fortunate news. I will place a notice in the *Gazette* as soon as we return to London."

* * *

Dinner passed as a celebration. The assembled party offered toasts and all good wishes. Smiles and laughter reached their lips, but one would have to read the eyes to know the truth.

While Leighton offered his congratulations, his eyes glittered with aversion. He had only himself to thank. He had practically driven her into the bastard's arms. He had come this weekend to end that possibility and instead had brought it about, unseconded.

Angel never once looked at Leighton. She could not. Her heart was about to break. She watched her future husband while he happily entertained his guests. He looked marvelously handsome and happy.

Mary Beth sat with a glowering expression. She managed a smile for the toast, but she knew instinctively this was wrong—all wrong—for Angel.

Lord Stewart felt satisfied that he had done well by Angel. She readily agreed when he first sought her wishes concerning the betrothal. He was glad to see her wed where she desired.

The Duchess of de Aubrey smiled sweetly, but her heart was heavy. She wished she knew Lady Harlan well enough to speak to her about marrying when your heart is not engaged. She recognized Lady Harlan's earlier expressions when she looked at Leighton. My heavens, pride makes fools of us all. They were meant for each other. There was nothing she could do unless . . . She toyed with several ideas.

The dowager Duchess of Albrion sat with resignation. The dowry was convincing and the child could be managed. It was acceptable, for there was no one worthy of her son. This chit would have to do. She was sure she could train her in the necessary duties.

When the evening finally came to an end, it was not too soon for any member attending.

18

Dear Libby,

Grandfather is gratified, for I am to be engaged to the Duke of Albrion. You will agree, when you meet him, that he is a noble gentleman. You must come up for the wedding. No date has been set, and the announcement will be made as soon as the duke returns to London.

We traveled to Marlefort to meet his mother and, I imagine, to receive her approval. I am not too sure how delighted his mother is, but then I have the distinct feeling few, if any, could quite come up to the touch. She has consented and the duke seems quite content. I am not sure how deep his affections are, but then that is not important as long as he amiable.

Quite by accident, I happened into Lord L———'s bedroom. He was the perfect gentleman—well, almost. He did kiss me. It is a great pity he does not seem inclined to wed.

I send my love and affection. Burn this letter.

Angel

* * *

Sending Jeanne off to post her letter to Libby, Angel climbed back into bed and closed her eyes. She had been listless and downcast for two days, and the dark-blue funk seemed to grow only worse. The duke had returned to town, but she was not well enough to see him. She was having terrifying thoughts about marrying him and not the nerve to halt the events already under way. To cry off from an engagement was paramount to her death sentence. Not that she cared, but Grandfather did. That was the deciding factor. He had cared for her like a mother hen; gruff and bluff, he had shielded her from the world of petty remarks as she grew up.

The engagement had been placed in the *Gazette*, and congratulations were pouring in along with myriad invitations. Angel declined them all, saying she was not well. Something had to be done, and she would do it. For now she hid in retreat; later she would take some kind of action, but what action?

Mary Beth did not know what to make of this uncharacteristic behavior and sent for the doctor, who declared Angel had some kind of ague, ordered some foul-tasting medicine, and advised confinement in bed for a few days.

Skeptical of the diagnosis, Mary Beth fretted. Angel, despite her fragile appearance, was as healthy as a horse. The child was never sick. She suspected it had something to do with the betrothal and Angel's attachment to Lord Leighton. She decided to find out.

Entering Angel's darkened room, she went to sit next to her on the bed. "Angel, you must be truthful with me. Are you unhappy?"

"Oh, Mary Beth, I fear I've made a terrible mistake that cannot be undone. They'll all think I'm just like my mother," she cried, and the held-in tears flowed like a damn broken. She cried in Mary Beth's arms until she subsided into hiccups.

"Angel, why did you consent?"

"Because everyone one wants me to marry well, and Leighton doesn't want to marry—at least, not me!" Her tears flowed again.

Mary Beth held her, rocked her, and shushed her. "Leighton?"

"Oh, yes, Leighton. I followed a light in the hidden passage. I think the duke was sneaking into the duchess's bedroom. I ended up in Lord Leighton's room and he kissed me. That's all he did . . . he kissed me."

"It's all right, dear. It's all right. I'll fix it. I didn't follow my heart once and have lived years of regret. The same shall not befall you. Rest, dear. I'll see what I can do, but you must promise to follow my instructions to the letter."

"Oh, dear, dear Mary Beth. How could you manage it? A betrothal is sacred. I'll be ostracized if I break off—"

"Well, you have been more than a handful, you know. Don't despair. You rest. Do not mention what you have told me to anyone. I must contrive a plan, but I'll have to think this through. We'll find a way. You're not without tenacity, and we'll manage."

"I vow I'll do whatever you say."

"That's my Angel, now rest, dear. Sleep. It will do you good, for you will need your strength as well as your acting skills to get through this one."

Angel obeyed, and having temporarily placed her fate in her loving aunt's capable hands, she drifted off into a deep sleep, which had been so elusive since returning from Marlefort.

Mary Beth rose and quietly left the room. Pausing, she stood a moment in the corridor, deep in thought. A glimmer of an idea brought forth a nefarious smile, which turned the corners of the lips on an otherwise paragon of spinster virtue.

After carefully thinking through her plans, Mary Beth sent a note asking to call on the Duchess of de Aubrey at precisely eleven o'clock concerning a matter of the utmost importance. Next, she sought her father in his study.

"Father, I am worried about Angel's happiness, and I am embarking on a plan to secure it. I need your cooperation, without questions."

"What do you mean 'without questions?' " he asked, taken aback at so unusual a request.

"Exactly that. I want you to go down to the country today. Tomorrow I shall send Angel to you. She is dreadfully unhappy."

He stared at his daughter, the one he had unwisely demanded his will concerning her happiness. That had been a dreadful mistake. Silently he sat, musing on the past and weighing the future.

"Do you trust me to right this grievous wrong about to blight our Angel's life?"

He nodded. "I'll leave within the hour and entrust you to whatever is necessary. See that she's safely escorted."

"I will, and if all does not go well, I shall bring her down myself."

"Mary Beth, you know I never meant to—"

"Father, that is past. Behind us. Let me make Angel's future all that we hope for her."

Mary Beth knew it was an almost-impossible task for her father to hand over the reins in this instant, because he never trusted anyone but himself. He was making a supreme concession. She smiled and placed a kiss on his bald head.

"Don't fear, I shall manage a skillful extrication."

"You take after me, I've no doubt." He chuckled.

Mary Beth sighed with relief: her most difficult hurdle had just been overcome. The rest had to be as easy as falling off a fence by comparison.

Dressed in her usual serviceable brown serge, Mary Beth was graciously received by the Duchess of de Aubrey.

"What help can I offer you, Lady Stewart?" the duchess asked, kindly bidding Mary Beth to be seated.

Mary Beth sat, folded her hands, and proceeded to tell her.

The lovely silvery laugh gleefully echoed in the room. "Lady Stewart, you are quite right. I am delighted to assist you. I shall ring for tea, and you must direct the words I am to write to the Duke of Albrion. It will give me much pleasure," she said with a devilish and delighted grin as she rang for a servant.

Mary Beth returned home in time to bid her father good-bye. "I will send Angel tomorrow, and remember I love you," she said to her totally surprised father.

"Ahem, er, yes. Do send her, safely now," he said gruffly, and paused to smile. "I don't know what you're up to, but you have my blessings," he said, and was gone. Calling last-minute orders, Lord Stewart waved to his daughter, feeling somehow as if all was well and in order. Takes after me, she does, he thought with satisfaction as he entered his crested coach for the journey to Farnham Manor.

Mary Beth thrust off her hat, gloves, and jacket and hurried to Angel's room.

"Darling, I've decided to send you down to the country. Father has already left on some urgent business or some such thing. So, it would be just the thing. We will say you have gone to Farnham Manor to enjoy the lovely weather and to recover. I shall take care of things here and follow as soon as I am able to get there."

Angel was so surprised, she sat up, suddenly looking vastly improved. "You mean, go home? Not stay in London? Why didn't you send me with Grandfather? I don't have to see the duke to tell him I've changed my mind? He scares me, Mary Beth. Truly, I've just come to realize, there's something about him—"

"Yes, dear. I understand, but now you must direct your packing. I didn't send you with Father because timing is important. You will have to leave early tomorrow morning. By ten, to be sure."

"Ten? Why ten? Anytime is fine for me. I'll leave at six."

"No, ten. Now I'll call in the maids and you direct us in what you wish to take," Mary Beth insisted.

"I don't really care what I take."

"You will, dear. Let us choose what is most charming," Mary Beth said, and rang for the maids.

"Mary Beth, you're treating me like a child. I'm behaving like one, am I? Bemoaning a fate most young ladies would envy."

Mary Beth turned to Angel with fury on her face. "Listen to me, my love. You have done everything to please those you thought you should. You have overcome your mother's indiscretion and, in doing so, given up the lively, impetuous young lady you truly are. To tell the truth, I miss the old Angel, the one who laughed, teased, and sang the day through. I can't say I like the mousy little maid you've shown society. I have been a part of this transformation, and as things have turned out, it was wrong."

"Mary Beth, you shock me. That is exactly what you have done. You bent to their will."

"Precisely, and that will not befall you. By all the saints above, you will not wither on a vine as I," Mary Beth said with a fierceness that silenced Angel into immediate acquiescence.

"Indeed, I shall go to Farnham Manor tomorrow, at ten o'clock." Angel smiled for the first time in days. Life came back into her eyes and relief filled her heart. Home, she was going home. She would sort out the mess when she got there, but for now, she would allow Mary Beth to dictate her direction. Her aunt seemed to be the only one who knew what she was doing.

Mary Beth, dressed in her servant's cloak, scurried along the same route Jeanne had taken two months before. She was unaware of this fact, of course, nor was she as frightened as poor Jeanne had been. Scurried was not precisely the manner in which she covered the streets to Lord Leighton's. She marched with a firm purposeful step, and no one would have dared to interfere.

She reached her destination and raised the knocker with a firm, loud clang. Once again, the footman opened the door to an early-morning caller. Another lady's maid with a note, he supposed; he held out his hand.

Mary Beth stepped into the doorway, pushing the surprised servant aside. "Inform Lord Leighton that Lady Mary Beth Stewart is here to speak with him. If he should choose not to see me, tell him I shall call him out."

She was amazed at the few minutes it took for Lord Leighton to appear, and a fleeting smile came to her lips. She watched him swiftly cross the foyer, still, if you can imagine such a thing, adjusting his attire. His hair was tousled and she studied his face. There was concern in his expression and his eyes. He was truly a fair and handsome man. A bit too good-looking for her taste; they are always the devil to deal with. Still, perhaps there was substance here. She was about to find out.

"Lady Stewart, what ever can be amiss?" He was filled with foreboding. This lady would never call upon a gentleman unless doomsday was imminent. He thought something had happened to Angel. Oh, God, he prayed, not so . . . "Is Angel—I mean, Lady Harlan well?"

"That is why I have called. May I speak to you privately?"

"But of course, this way please. My study," he

said, ushering her into the room while his servant stood and stared.

Mary Beth turned to face the marquess. "Tell me, my lord, exactly your feeling concerning my niece."

19

If trepidation, anticipation, and hope can bring a total of happiness, then Lord Leighton was the happiest he had been for many years. The anticipation prompted his early rising, leaving him ample time. Hope was the youthful joy that brought the radiant warmth to his expression, which had attracted the adulation he had received all his adult life. The difference today was that his direction was no longer aimless. He knew, for the first time in his life, exactly what he wanted. The trepidation he hid deep within his heart, and he prayed that he would be successful.

His valet watched his employer with interest as he assisted his lordship into his impeccable superfine coat. He noted his lordship whistled a merry tune and seemed to have lost the downcast attitude that had uncharacteristically been part of his countenance of late. He was gratified to see his lordship so happy.

"Please have my horse saddled and brought around by eight," Lord Leighton requested. "Also pack some fresh linens, as I might not return this evening."

At precisely eight o'clock, Lord Leighton, looking marvelously fit, mounted his horse for an early-morning call on Major-General MacDougal. A smile played on Ward's lips for this day's adventure, which was about to begin.

Ushered into the dining room, where Duncan was seated at his usual, ample repast, Leighton greeted him with a frown.

"Good morning, Duncan. I am here to bid you good-bye for a while," he said with an edge of agitation in his voice.

"Gad, man, what ever is amiss? You seem agitated."

"Do I? No. I am . . . Well, that is . . ." He let his voice fade.

Duncan rose. "Can I be of service?"

"No. I only ask that you back me up when the news gets out."

"What news?"

"I'm not at liberty to say," Leighton said, trying not to smile in order to keep the sense of impending doom he was trying to convey.

"You're here to ask me back you up on something you can't tell me about?"

"Exactly, you're a stout fellow. I knew I could depend on you," Leighton said with a faltering smile, and shook Duncan's hand vigorously. "Well, I must be off. Happiness is about to be mine," Ward said, and turned on his heel and simply departed.

Duncan stood dumbfounded. My GOD, the man's gone daft, he thought, and sat down to a breakfast he no longer wanted.

Leaving MacDougal's residence, Lord Leighton directed his stallion to the Great North Road and the Swan and Rose.

At the same time Lord Leighton headed out of

London, the Earl *Duke* of Albrion finished his dressing.
He smelled of bay rum and his locks were combed
à la Brutus. His tight-fitting coat showed off his
manly physique, and he smiled with anticipation.
Fingering the lightly perfumed note, he ran it past
his nose and took a deep breath. Ah, the lady was
magnificent; he couldn't wait to bury his face in the
tumbling mass of curls he now pictured draped
over lace pillows. The duke was ever the roué, the
pillows in his fantasy, of course, were lavishly
laced. Placing his beaver hat on his head, he left his
house to climb into his waiting carriage.

"To the Great North Road and the King's Arms,"
he commanded.

The Duchess of de Aubrey stepped languidly out
of her bath and began her toilette. Her maid
assisted her into a beautiful rose traveling dress
that showed off her creamy skin to perfection. She
sat down to the ministrations of her hairdresser.
It would not do to be on time; it is always best to
keep a gentleman waiting. She smiled with the same
expression that had crossed Lady Stewart's face the
day before. It was pure knavery.

Widowhood was proving to be more interesting
every day. But then widowhood from the Duke of
de Aubrey was paramount to being freed from
Newgate.

"Call my carriage around, please," the duchess
ordered.

The house had been in a turmoil all morning.
Mary Beth ran breathlessly about, ordering all the
packing of the trunks and urging her niece to hurry.

"Mary Beth, why the rush? There is no reason to
press so," Angel complained, for she was not as
anxious as her aunt.

"Dear, you must get up. I want you at Farnham before nightfall," she said.

"And so I shall be," Angel replied as she placed her bonnet on her fair curls. She wore a white muslin dress with a robin's-egg-blue pelisse. Her hat was of the same blue, with a cluster of creamy roses. She looked as fragile and lovely as the bluebells now gracing the garden.

Mary Beth and Helmsley escorted Angel and Jeanne to the waiting carriage. "Good-bye, dear." Mary Beth hugged and kissed her niece. "Remember, I love you very much. Do make yourself happy, and I shall be there to join you just as soon as possible."

"You're coming this week, aren't you?"

"Yes, dear, I'll be there as soon as I take care of all that needs to be done."

"Even—"

"Yes, dear, even that matter, and to your satisfaction, I assure you."

The coachman cracked his whip and the carriage was off with a start. Angel sat back and sighed. However was her aunt going to get her out of the betrothal? Mary Beth had been very secretive, saying it was best she didn't know just yet. Angel had agreed because she herself was without an idea on the matter. She was terrified of making a scandal just as her mother had.

Mary Beth lifted her skirts and ran back into the hall. She called out for a bath to be prepared and went to pen a note. Sprinkling sand over the quickly written missive, she called for Hemsley.

"Helmsley, come into the study a moment. I have some orders I wish to discuss."

He obeyed with a decided interest, for this usually quiet young woman had been in a state of frenzied activity all morning. Knowing something

was astir, he left the study to call Jamison, the
footman. "Here, take this note to Major-General
Duncan MacDougal. It is of the utmost urgency,"
the butler commanded.

Mary Beth again picked up her skirts and
mounted the steps two at a time, to the shocked
amazement of Helmsley, who had been placed as
sentry at the front door.

Her toilette completed, Mary Beth stood and
stared at her reflection. Her maid was beside
herself with praise and exaltation. Gone was the
bun at the nape of her neck. In its place was a mass
of nut-brown curls. Mary Beth had even brushed
a hint of rouge on her cheeks, though she hardly
needed any, from all the excitement. That excitement brought fire to her hazel eyes and she looked
smashing.

She was about to put on her hat when a knock
sounded on her chamber door. Dora opened it to
a flustered Helmsley. "Lord Hatton has called," he
informed her in stilted tones.

Great heavens, no, not now, Mary Beth thought.
She hurried past the butler and scurried down the
steps. She must put Hatton off without his knowing
Angel had gone.

"Good morning, Lord Hatton," Mary Beth said,
entering the room with a fixed smile.

Lord Hatton's eyes almost bugged out of his head.
He hardly recognized Lady Stewart. She looked
years younger and positively fetching. His mouth
hung open.

"Angel has gone to purchase some—" Mary
Beth's words were interrupted by Helmsley's loud
voice.

"Lady Elizabeth Stanton has called to see Lady
Angel," he announced, with an accent on the name
"Angel."

Libby entered the room with a swift stride and anxious expression. "I've come to rescue Angel," she announced as soon as she had crossed the threshold.

Mary Beth almost fainted. "How delightful," she fairly screamed. "Let me introduce you to Lord Hatton, dear."

Libby dropped a quick curtsy and looked to Mary Beth.

"Lord Hatton, do be seated. I have an errand I wish you to perform. Would you be so kind as to wait a moment while I speak to Miss Stanton? Come, dear, let us go into the study. I am anxious to ask you how your mother is," Mary Beth said, grasping the young lady by her sleeve and all but dragging her from the room. As soon as they entered the hall, Mary Beth raised her finger to her lips to silence the girl and led her to the study.

"Whatever are you doing here?" Mary Beth hissed as she closed the door.

"I've come to save Angel. She's going to marry the wrong man."

"Does your father know you're here?"

"No, I slipped away during chapel and bribed Edwards to take me to the stage coach."

"You came by common coach?" Mary Beth said, nearly faint by now.

"Yes, I've got to save Angel. She loves Leighton, I can tell by her letters, and when she got into his bedroom, I thought—"

"Good heavens above, who else knows?"

"I'm sure no one," the flustered girl replied.

"Well, rest assured I am making arrangements for Angel. I will not allow her to wed the duke. Now, we must return you home. Can you make an excuse for your father?"

"You mean, lie?"

"Yes, I mean lie. No one must know about Leighton until—"

"I'll tell him I was homesick, or some such thing."

"Good, now let us go back to the salon," Mary Beth said, opening the door. "Now, not a word."

Libby trailed after Mary Beth Stewart with a perplexed look upon her pretty face.

Lord Hatton rose when the ladies entered. He was very taken by this comely young lady. He offered what he hoped was his most gracious bow.

"Lord Hatton, Lady Stanton is Viscount Stanton's daughter, and she has just missed seeing Angel. Would you be so kind as to escort her home? She has just come up from school."

Mary Beth knew it was highly improper for a young lady not yet out of school to be so escorted, but there it was, nothing else to do. Time was growing too short.

"I should be most delighted. I'll see her safely home," Hatton said in his best authoritarian, masculine voice.

Libby was impressed with this gentleman of the first stare, and she smiled. A pair of dimples peeked out at each corner of her mouth and she fluttered her eyes, just as Angel had told her.

Hatton was dazzled as he took her arm.

Angel was right! It's easy, and Libby turned another bewitching smile upon the young man.

Mary Beth watched them leave, sighed relief, then scurried up the stairs to get her bonnet and bandbox.

Lord Hatton handed Lady Stanton into his curricle and climbed in next to her. Deftly snapping the reins, he set his pair into motion. He had to pull in

when a coach accompanied by four scarlet-coated
Horse Guards rounded the corner at an unsafe
speed.

"You see, you can never count on the other fellow
to drive sensibly," he said mildly, wanting to swear
an oath at the fool who would travel at such a break-
neck speed in the city.

"My, what a lovely matched set of bays," Libby
said, "and you handle them so masterfully."

Lord Hatton sat a little taller. "Some say I'm
quite a whipster, but then, that's not for me to say,"
he replied with a modest expression.

"Oh, but I'm sure you're widely admired," she
said, and smiled up at him. Angel is right, this is
vastly more fun than school.

"Will you be coming to London next year?"
Hatton asked.

"Yes, I'm to make my come-out next spring," she
said.

"I hope you will allow me to show you about."

"Why, Lord Hatton, I should be delighted," Libby
said with the charm of an experienced flirt.

A little high praise was all he needed to come to
the front. He knew the next Season would find him
among the Corinthians of his set. He would look
forward to calling on so intelligent a young lady.

Lord Hatton was not aware that this young
"intelligent" lady had skipped out of chapel, bribed
a groomsman, and traveled on public coach, all
without her parents' knowledge. The alarm had
probably already gone out on her being missing.

"Please do not get out of the carriage. I think it
best if I go in alone. I do look forward to seeing you
next spring," Libby said as she practically leapt
from the curricle. She was in enough trouble
without explaining Lord Hatton. Happily, she
waved as she mounted the steps to her father's

London house. It was encouraging to already have an admirer.

Lord Hatton tipped his hat and said, "Until next year, Lady Stanton." Cracking the whip smartly, he was off in a flourish of flashing hooves, hoping he had properly impressed Lady Stanton.

20

The coach, escorted by four scarlet-coated Horse Guardsmen, halted before the front of Lord Stewart's town house. Helmsley, who had been on the lookout, came hurrying out of the house.

"Her ladyship will be with you presently," Helmsley informed Major-General MacDougal as he stepped from the coach.

Duncan MacDougal placed his hat upon his head, eyeing the butler with a questioning look. He crossed his arms, leaned against the coach, and waited nervously.

The door swung opened and Mary Beth stepped out, accompanied by two footmen carrying one large bandbox and another, smaller hatbox. Dressed to the nines, she looked marvelous, the epitome of the fashionable lady. Her outrageous bonnet sported large, curling plumes, which fluttered as she walked down the steps to where MacDougal stood.

It was *déjà vu* for Duncan as he watched with a pounding heart and painful memories. A soldier of the empire, and he stood fighting back tears. He stepped gallantly forward and took her hand, gloved in sapphire-blue doeskin.

Mary Beth raised her eyes to his and sent a sweet, secretive smile. Their eyes met and the lost years vanished. Assisting her into the carriage, he climbed in behind her as Helmsley put up the stairs and shut the door.

"Do not wait up, Helmsley. I may go on to Farnham Manor. I shall send back a messenger if I do."

"Very good, my lady," the butler replied, a slight tremor in his voice for Lady Mary Beth. He was old, and he remembered.

Major-General MacDougal gave the orders and the coach and troop were off in a flurry of clacking hooves. Sitting back, he turned to Mary Beth, "You are lovely, Mary Beth. Just as I remember so many years ago."

"Duncan, do not put the accent on 'so many years ago.' I'll feel quite middle-aged if you do, and somehow, today, I feel young again."

"You are a bonny lass, just as you were when I asked you to marry me." There was rancor in his voice.

Mary Beth knew she must get the conversation on another track. No recriminations now. "Duncan, I sent for you because I need your help."

"How may I help? You've said Angel's run off with Leighton. Are we to hunt them down and bring them back?"

Mary Beth was silent; maybe this wasn't going to be as easy as she had hoped. "I think we must try to catch them; we don't want another scandal."

"That's why I brought the contingency with me. I can send them ahead to scout the road. I would have done so myself, but you insisted in coming along."

"Duncan, she could hardly return in your carriage, with four soldiers," Mary Beth said.

"No, I suppose not. Well, which way do you think they went? I must give the coachman directions."

"Doesn't everyone go to Gretna Green?"

Duncan chuckled. "Scotland, aye, lass, that they do. A fairland 'tis, Scotland. I wish you could see it," he said.

"So do I, Duncan."

The major-general called to the coachman to take the Great North Road.

They sat in silence for a while.

"They can't have much of a start, for Leighton was around about half-past eight this morning. Two to three hours, I should think. Of course, Leighton's a master at the ribbons. If he's bound to make time, he'll be hard to catch. I've got a jehu on the box who can catch them, and Leighton will not expect me to come after him," Duncan said with regret. Leighton had asked Duncan to back him up, and here he was in hot pursuit.

"You're against Leighton for Lady Angel?"

"Not if she loves him."

"Then why chase them?"

"I don't want a hole-in-the-wall marriage. She has overcome enough scandal."

"Frankly, it's not Leighton's style to run off with a girl. It strikes me as out of character."

Mary Beth laughed. "I think many of us are out of character today. No, I'm wrong, perhaps we're our true selves at last."

He looked at Mary Beth and remembered the last time he had held her. "You're a bonny lass, Mary Beth. How is it you never married?"

She turned her radiant face to him. "Thank you, Duncan. I never found anyone else. How is it you never married?"

"Been too busy, and I never looked for anyone else."

Silence again fell over the couple. The coach continued its race through the streets and out into the countryside.

The Duchess of de Aubrey was ushered into the private dining room of the King's Arms by a bowing and scraping hostler, who was grateful for such quality patrons and the half-crown tip for his discretion. She moved with the smooth elegant grace that was bred into one, not learned.

The Duke of Albrion caught his breath at the sight of her. Rushing to greet her, he raised her hand to his lips. "I thought the time would never come, the wait was an eternity."

"You speak such pretty words, your grace," she said, and laughed.

"No, 'tis true," he vouched.

"Yes," she said, "I suppose it is." Her eyes danced with merry mischief, which our foolish, infatuated lover interpreted as naughtiness.

"Madeleine, you're so exciting and beautiful. I counted the moments," he said, drawing her to him.

"Your grace, you move too fast," she said as she gracefully slipped away.

"Call me William," he said.

"Yes, William, but you must tell me why you are here when you are to wed Lady Harlan?"

"She's just to be my wife, a marriage of convenience. She's not as exciting as you are. I've got to have a wife, but she's not the sort to stir my passions. I need someone like you, exciting," he said, heartfelt emotion in his voice. He moved to draw her again into his arms. "You fit me so well, you belong in my arms," he said, lowering his lips to hers.

She allowed him to kiss her. His warm brown eyes glowed with passion and he smiled tenderly at her.

"William, I'm not the sort to engage in a tiresome liaison. I need a lasting love, as do most ladies," she said, and raised her beautiful eyes to him.

"I'll leave her for you. She doesn't mean that much to me," he said, pulling her close to him."

"You'll cry off?" she asked with feigned pleasure. "Then think what an exciting future we might have!"

"I'll do it," he exclaimed. The coward in him would never allow him to be placed in disesteem. He was a manipulator of people for his own ends and fabricated self-image. His facade never matched his soul, so he'd find a way that made Lady Harlan look bad, not him. He was a master at making and believing his own lies.

"Good! Then, it is settled. Write me a letter to take to Lady Harlan, and we'll go away for a while. I have a wonderful house in Brighton," she said, sidling up to him and reaching to place her arms around his neck. "Besides, I suspect Lady Harlan loves Leighton," she said, knowing the sting of his being second-best in all things would rankle him.

Corners spat. "He deserves her if she's stupid enough to have him."

A short while later, Madeleine left the King's Arms with the duke's written cry-off to the engagement and the smile of a victor. Hell would freeze over before Lord Corners ever crossed her threshold. As far as she was concerned, the worm no longer existed.

The Duke of Albrion stood at the window and watched her carriage roll away, holding empty promises of future delights as redeemable as

Spanish coin. He smiled with a satisfaction he was soon to find had no foundation.

Two of the Horse Guards who had been scouting ahead returned to the general's carriage. "Sir, we've located Lord Leighton's carriage outside the Swan and Rose."

Duncan turned to Mary Beth. "Our quarry is at hand. What do you propose to do?"

As they rounded the bend, the courtyard of the inn was clearly visible and Mary Beth could see Lord Stewart's coach being guided to the side of the inn.

"Duncan, what say we let them work out their decision on their own?" She placed her hand on his arm and looked into his eyes. Longing and love sparkled from the golden-hazel eyes and an expression of devotion glowed on her face.

"I agree, have from the beginning. I only wanted to please you. Leighton will do right by her, and I'm sure as one can be, it's April and May between them. All one had to do was look at the lovesick couple. Then what do we do now?"

"Duncan, I'd love to see Scotland, especially Gretna Green," she coyly said, and even batted her lashes.

Duncan laughed. "Are ye being so bold as to propose to me? Run away like a schoolgirl, would ye?"

"To the ends of the earth, Duncan. I should never have listened to Father, but then it was during the time Evelyn ran off."

"And I a mere enlisted man with little prospects. Well, you're as bold as baggage and I'll take you to Gretna Green, then on to meet my mother. She'll perish with delight at so bonny a wife I've managed to capture. Although it should be more accurately placed as your having captured me," he quipped.

"I suppose you'll brag all our days that it was I who tricked you into running off and marrying me."

"But of course, my love. 'Tis the truth, and I'm a man of honor," he said, sweeping her into his arms and planting a very thorough kiss on her eager lips. "I'm the happiest of men. We'll know more than most, for we lost much by allowing all those years to slip away."

"Duncan, I know what we'll do. We'll love each other twice as much and make up each day," she said, snuggling into his arms.

"Now there's a promise a man can live with and honor with equal enthusiasm." Leaning out the window, he called to his men, "We're going on to the border. You can return to London or witness a wedding," he called.

"We'll witness a wedding, one that had a military escort all the way," his corporal called back.

Duncan settled back in the squabs with Mary Beth in his arms. "One way only, after that we're on our own," he said, and kissed her again.

Angel entered the inn with Jeanne in tow. "Our axle, I'm told, needs repair, so we wish to secure a room," she said.

The ruddy-faced hostler bowed and offered an appropriate response of dismay at the inconvenience to the lady of quality.

"I'll show your maid my best room and allow her to settle you in. Perhaps, the problem can quickly be righted. I have a private dining parlor. Please, this way. My wife will show your abigail to the bedchamber."

As he had been handsomely paid to do, he escorted her to the private dining parlor in which a gentleman had waited several hours.

Angel walked through the doorway and saw Lord Leighton standing by the window. She was surprised to see him there. Yet, deep within her heart the inevitability of fate seemed to take the surprise away. His eyes never left her face as she slowly walked toward him.

"Can you forgive me for having your coach waylaid? I had to see you and plead my case," he said, and his smile reached his eyes and her soul.

"I think, my lord, I shall reserve my judgment until I hear your case."

He ran his hand through his hair and nervously began, hoping against hope his plea was convincing. "Angel, you have been in my thoughts from the time I rescued your silly shoe. I will tell you I resisted my growing *tendre* with the diligence of a man bound for hell. My life has not been exemplary, and I am not proud of that fact. I had grown tired of the mendacity of men and became the very object of my contempt, cynical and without hope or belief in the authenticity of love. I was not sure it even existed, I have seen little among our contemporaries."

"Lord Corners included?" she asked.

He looked at her sharply, then smiled. "Yes, he is a rake, but you see, so was I. How could I have presented myself, no better and much worse than most?"

"I would say, my lord, that you had not presented yourself . . . that is."

"I felt like a hypocrite. Then you showed me what a pure, unselfish thing love could be, and I trembled with fear. I knew from whence I came, not knowing why I stood on the threshold of something else. How could I ask you to become my wife?"

Angel smiled. "How could you, indeed?"

"Angel, you're a devil, you're not making this easy."

"What should I then say, my lord?"

"Don't say anything and just listen to the plea of a reformed rascal. I love you. I witnessed your courage against all odds. You have tenacity and a sense of the ridiculous. Life could be nothing but an endless unfolding adventure. I need you. My devotion makes a mockery of all that I once believed—or rather, didn't believe—and I fear if you say no, I am lost forever. Never have I, nor never will I, love like this again." Making no move toward her, holding steady and watching her every expression, he stood with trembling hope.

"Sounds like a bit of blackmail, Leighton."

He laughed and stepped forward to take her in his arms. "You're correct, but you are not without affection for me. I can feel it. Albrion will only bring you pain and sorrow. Marry me, my Angel, and give me heaven," he said, and bent to kiss her.

His kiss was warm and loving; all his pent-up hopes and fears were placed in it, as if to capture her forever. Her senses reeled. She was equally in love and had given up any hope of the heretofore unattainable dream.

He kissed her neck and whispered sweet words. "Say yes, Angel, and save a sinner."

She laughed. "Angels are meant to save sinners, and I shall be no exception. I say yes, Leighton, with a glad and happy heart."

He picked her up around the waist and whirled her around. "I can't believe my good fortune. I can't believe you'll have me. Angel, I vow to make you happy. I never thought to find such happiness. I didn't believe in life and the goodness of such a possibility."

"Lord Leighton, I think it is your turn to be quiet. Perhaps I've acquiesced too quickly. I need more convincing," she said with a merry, teasing, and provocative laugh.

He brought her tight against his chest and covered her with a dozen kisses. "Is that convincing, my love?"